Goblin Fruit

Goblin Fruit

and Other Curiosities

Stories

SHERRI COOK WOOSLEY

Interior Illustrations by Joshua Ormido

an imprint of

ARC
MANOR
Rockville, Maryland

ISBN: 978-1-64973-185-2

www.PhoenixPick.com

Phoenix Pick Edition, October 2025.

Published by Phoenix Pick
an imprint of Arc Manor
P. O. Box 10339
Rockville, MD 20849-0339
www.ArcManor.com

Thank you to Lyn for convincing me that readers would want to participate in the strange stories in my head

Thank you to the readers who can't say "no" to Goblin Fruit.

Contents

BAKE ME A CAKE

She pours the warm Goblin fruit drizzle; the chocolate shell melts to reveal the inside.

Bake Me a Cake

The long tent stands alone in an idyllic grassy field, a flag with a triquetra—three arched ovals inside a golden ring—flapping in the gentle breeze. Inside, the tent is furnished with cooking stations that face a long table; behind it loom three Fey thrones made of entwined branches. The castle stands at the head of the field, straddling the line between mortal and Fairy, while the foot of the field disappears into thick forest. Alana struggles to breathe as panic beats bird wings in her chest. Back in the village, she is something special as she creates delicate pastries and makes deliveries on the back of Ol' Betsy. But she didn't choose to come to the castle, didn't choose to vie for the position of Royal Baker. She is here because her father boasted of her talent and now, in one day, her life has changed.

Falcon, the Fey attendant with dandelion yellow hair, takes a place near the thrones and stands at attention.

Two stations are already claimed. One by a human boy who looks to be about twenty, the same age as her. He's attractive with long fingers and a constellation of freckles across his light brown skin. His shirt sleeves are pushed up unevenly.

Noticing her look, he nods. "Pick a station." Then, as an after-thought, "I'm Henry."

1

The human woman at the station behind Henry's is older than Alana and has thin lips that almost disappear as she anxiously presses them together. Most of her red hair is pulled into a bun but shorter pieces curl near her cheeks and hide her expression when she leans forward. Catching Alana's eye, she says, "Grace."

Falcon snorts from her position.

"My true name," Grace teases. "And I just toss it about."

Alana blinks. She hasn't seen many Fey and mortal interactions and doesn't understand the joke. Her village was too far east to be significantly affected by the war between Fey and mortals. Riding to the castle yesterday, Alana had been shocked by the abandoned fields and burned buildings surrounding the capital. Most disturbing, the head of mortal King Robert II was displayed on the city gate. Blood still dripping from his neck though it has been five years. Fey magic to quiet any human rebellions.

Alana claims a station and squats down to check her brick oven, already warm. Leaning against the warmth, her hands run over her apron. The garment is embroidered with pictures of dough in various shapes: pretzel, loaf, knots, and twists. Alana's mother made it before she died and wearing it makes Alana feel connected. The memory of her mother evokes more comforting images of the village bakery. Measuring flour by scraping the flat of a blade across the top, whipping milk and sugar to create a firm texture, letting dough proof long enough to create air pockets. As confidence returns, Alana's shoulders relax. She acknowledges a desire to win, not just because she has been told to compete. Somewhere within she acknowledges a desire that has been dormant: a desire to see beyond her village. Her father is amiable but lazy and the villagers eat her cookies in three bites without noticing whether the icing is buttercream or royal. Today, however, she will have experts judging.

Henry moves around his station, impatient.

Alana is used to small talk, the kind that passes time while customers wait in line. "Back home my wooden spoon has a burned handle. Everything here is so new."

"Human-made is best," Henry says. "When did you get here?"

"Yesterday."

"Cutting it close."

"I didn't intend—" Alana doesn't know how to finish. The painful memory returns. Standing outside the bakery. Prince Rondo and Princess Morwen staring down from their milk white steeds. Papa boasting that she is the best baker in the realm. His palm shoving her forward. Morwen's cruel green eyes narrowing. The order for Alana to mount Ol' Betsy without even a moment to pack.

Henry nods. He seems to understand there is more to the story. "You look exhausted."

"The singing last night kept me awake. It confused my dreams. Was it a banshee?"

"I didn't hear anything, but this place is twisted with magic. Don't trust it. Also," Henry points at Alana, "don't eat any of their food. Did anyone tell you that? One bite and you're trapped; you'll never be able to leave Fairy."

"I heard rumors." Alana chews the inside of her cheek.

Across the way, Grace folds her arms and shakes her hair back as she watches the castle steps.

Henry leans close to whisper, "Careful. I think that one's a sympathizer." Then he stiffens, his gaze locked.

Alana pivots. There! King Angus MacOg strides down to the tent followed by Princess Morwen and Prince Rondo. Prince Rondo's long hair is white like the down of a swan and he wears a striking red coat with a high collar. Antler buds poke through his hair on either side, visible when he glances at Grace and then quickly away.

In contrast to her twin, Morwen steps into the tent demanding admiration, hand on hip. Alana can't look away from her ivory skin and sharp cheekbones. Branches with blooming roses and sharp thorns have been braided into her glossy, dark hair and Alana tells herself not to touch her own plain braids in self-conscious reflex.

"Greetings, bakers." King Angus does not raise his voice, yet the sound carries.

They all sink down to honor him.

"Rise."

It is difficult to tell the king's age, although some say he is centuries old. As Alana straightens, she ignores the full antlers on top of his head to focus on his face. A hint of wrinkles fan from jaded eyes the same hue as Morwen's, although the king's are half-lidded as if he is falling asleep.

Falcon announces: "Today you will bake two loaves of bread: one savory and one sweet. One baker will be eliminated. You have until sunset."

"How do we get ingredients?" Alana asks.

"Name the ingredients and they will appear," Falcon says. "Begin."

The royal family sweeps back into the castle.

Wondering, Alana speaks into the air, "Flour." There is a shimmer, a breeze, and then a bag of flour sits on the counter. "Uh. I mean wheat flour. Please."

The bag wafts away and a bag of wheat flour appears, arriving with a thud that causes brown granules to puff into the air.

"Cauliflower. Turmeric. Red pepper. Bacon. Parmesan cheese." Each time she lists something, it appears. She doesn't need a recipe; she'll rely on her experience. Once she has the savory mixed, she'll make a peaches-and-cream bread. The sweet icing will be perfect for the warm weather. "Heavy cream, milk, sour cream."

As Alana measures the flour, she glances at Henry. "Why do you think we are here? I mean, why do Fey care about baking?"

"They don't. Truth is, Fey live long lives so they like to torture humans for entertainment." He punches the dough with wild abandon. "They should've stayed on their side of the hedge."

Across the aisle, Grace has dill, Asiago cheese, and what looks like deer meat. She grits her teeth, but doesn't respond.

Falcon walks laps around the outside of the tent.

For the savory, Alana will divide the dough into three parts and plait it like she did her hair this morning. Like Morwen's too. Alana shakes the thought away. She'll need to make the peaches-and-cream bread more sophisticated to keep herself in the competition. Deciding to twist the sweet bread into a circle, Alana separates eggs into yolks and whites.

When the sun is almost set, Falcon calls time. Princess Morwen and Prince Rondo reappear.

"Bakers," Rondo calls. "Exhibit your breads."

Alana places a garnish. Her breads are the best she's ever made, but she doesn't know if they will be good enough. Grace's sweet loaf is formed in the shape of a swan, dusted with powdered sugar for feathers.

Henry's loaves are the typical shape. Alana wants to wish him good luck, but Henry stares at the ground and mutters.

"My brother and I," says Princess Morwen, "are prepared to judge." She gestures to Henry. "You first."

He carries the baking paddle up to the table before the royals. Then he thrusts his hand into one of the loaves, ripping it open.

Alana frowns, not understanding.

"For Armagh," Henry screams, lunging across the table, a knife covered in crumbs aimed at Rondo.

"No," yells Grace. She rushes forward, arms extended as if she can drag Henry away from Rondo.

Falcon draws her blade.

But Morwen is faster. She raises her hand and snaps.

Henry hangs in the air mid-leap, body frozen, and the knife an inch from the prince's face. Henry's face remains twisted in an angry expression.

Alana can't make a sound. She's never seen magic like this before.

Grace stops halfway to the judging table and Morwen pierces her with a glare. "Remember your place, peasant."

Grace retreats, eyes on Prince Rondo.

Morwen lifts an eyebrow at Alana and then Grace. "Did either of you hide weapons in your bread?"

They shake their heads.

"Then you both move to the next level. Henry, you are eliminated."

"Anything to add, brother?"

Rondo shakes his head.

Morwen speaks words that Alana can't understand. Specks of light surround Henry. He crumples into himself and the knife clatters to the floor. Soft brown fur covers what used to be a man until a rabbit with long ears sits on the tent floor. The rabbit uses a back foot to scratch behind an ear and then hops away to the green grass.

"Tomorrow's challenge is to bake a cake that could be served at a royal function." Morwen seems unaffected by either the attack or her retaliation. "Both taste and presentation will count towards the final score."

5

Alana and Grace nod.

"However," Morwen says with a cruel expression in her beautiful eyes, "we'll make it more interesting. As we agreed, the human who wins shall have a position at the castle as Royal Baker and the other will be," she glances at the rabbit, "eliminated."

Sweat breaks out across Alana's forehead. She raises her hand like she is in school. She wants to object but she doesn't know the words to argue with royalty.

Princess Morwen smiles at Alana as she says, "Your father says you are the best baker. We shall see."

"However," Prince Rondo adds, "judging is blind."

Morwen and Rondo glare at each other.

"We are each," he says, "allowed to make rules."

"Fine," Morwen says. "I only wish mother were here to see."

Rondo swallows, but he holds Morwen's gaze as he nods.

Mother? Then Alana remembers that the queen was killed during the war and understands the painful barb between the siblings.

When the Fey leave, Alana collapses onto the stool. To the right, Ol' Betsy is in the pasture with the milk-white horses. She kicks at a Fey mare who gets too close and Alana laughs with a helpless kind of panic. This morning she wanted to win to show off her baking. Now she'll be turned into a rabbit if she fails.

Food, to Alana, is supposed to be about relationships, about sharing traditions and creating a special memory with other people. It is the way that Alana shows love and it is being twisted like a pretzel for this competition.

"What is Armagh?" she asks.

Grace clears her throat. "It's the ruined town outside the castle. The extremists say the Fey tied foxes together, set their tails on fire, and let them loose in the fields. But, it's not true. Well," she tilts her head, "they did burn the fields and salt them in retaliation King Robert II's poisoning of the streams. There were no foxes involved."

"How do you know?"

"I worked in the kitchen after the war when human refugees were allowed inside. I've seen mortals and Fey choose to work together to start rebuilding the castle." She shrugs one shoulder. "Of course, there's plenty of hate and blame on both sides."

"Is this competition about rebuilding or about animus?"

Grace snorts. "That's the question, isn't it?"

Alana rubs her forehead. This whole situation is absurd, a game for the Fey. "Why did the king agree to it?"

"King Angus MacOg is fair, but he's tired. I know what Henry said earlier, but the reason he crossed the hedge was because King Robert was poisoning the water. Fey kings are connected to the land. In a way it was self-defense. There are two sides to every story and the truth is somewhere in-between." Grace balls up a cleaning cloth. "King Angus wants to watch the twins interact with humans so he knows who to make his heir. But mortals need to learn too, like not eating Fey food, and the power of true names, and the ritual of gifts."

Alana has only heard of the geis against food, but doesn't want to admit this. She asks, "Ritual of gifts?"

"Every accepted gift must be reciprocated so it's very rude to offer a gift because it puts a Fey in your debt."

"I see." She didn't. It made friendship sound like a legalistic transaction. Alana knew the villagers and remembered who was allergic to nuts, kept a list of customer birthdays under the counter, and charged less to families who were having a rough time. That's what it meant to be a neighbor. "So will the royal family honor the terms of the competition or are they lying?"

"Fey can't lie." Grace looks surprised. "That's why they play word games and tell riddles."

"And what about the thing you were saying about 'true names' to Falcon earlier? Isn't that her name?"

"Those are public names. Sharing their true name is rare and intimate." An expression of regret appears and is gone before Alana can be certain. "Not something they'd ever do with a human."

Then Alana's stomach growls. She's been working with food all day but hasn't eaten.

"You can get dinner in the kitchen. Mortal food." Grace pushes away from the counter. "I'm sorry you were dragged here. I, at least, volunteered."

Alana stores that information to consider later. "We should probably go plan our cakes for tomorrow. Our lives depend on it."

She holds out a hand and is proud when it only shakes a little. "May the best baker win."

Grace shakes it. "May the best baker win." Her smile, too, trembles.

Alana's head throbs as she lays on the bed with eyes closed, replaying every moment since Papa's boast. She'd gone to the kitchen and eaten cheese and venison jerky, but now her stomach cramps with anxiety. Grace's bread would have beaten hers today. That meant tomorrow she could die and her village—her Papa—would never know what happened. Would Papa sell the bakery? She imagines the mural of her family being painted over, the painting on the back wall that showed her holding hands as she stood between her parents.

Her hand clutches her apron and her mother is in the room. Alana knows not to open her eyes or the dream or ghost or demon will leave. The familiar voice says, "I did not love your father but I married him so I could have you. And you are everything I ever wanted. Be clever, my daughter. You know how a recipe works but there is more to this test."

When the banshee begins her song, Alana opens her eyes to the empty room. Drifting like a sleepwalker, Alana stumbles out the door and follows the song deeper into the castle until it stops. She stands, lost in the darkness. There is a hallway to the left with windows that overlook a courtyard and a door to the right with warm light shining through the gap where it meets the floor. Soft voices come through the door.

Alana moves toward the light; her hand pushes the door. The room is similar to hers, except that Grace is sitting on the bed, naked. Her face is flushed, lips swollen, nipples tight. Wind blows in through a window that looks out on the tent of cooking stations— the curtains shake and a long strand of white hair hangs, gleaming in the candlelight.

"The s-s-song," Alana stammers. "Do you hear the song?"

"Get out," Grace yells, covering herself.

Alana spins around and runs down the hallway, gasping for breath at a window. Her palms press into the stones and her fingers splay open. There! In the courtyard, a figure in white lifts her throat toward the stars, and resumes her haunting lament. The music pulls at Alana and she is helpless to resist: she lifts her skirt and climbs through the open window into the night air.

The figure notices Alana and closes her mouth, but the eyes are unmistakable. Princess Morwen.

"Did I invite you?" Morwen's expression is savage. Alana is reminded of Mrs. Wilmer from the village, an older woman whose arthritis hurts so much that she'll snap at anyone who tries to help.

"Your song," Alana says, "makes me...sad." The words are too simple for how her heart feels laid bare.

"Do you think you understand pain, mortal? You are a mayfly, dying as soon as you are born. But my people should live for centuries." She emphasizes "should."

"You hate humans because your mother was killed in the war." Knowledge clicks. "That's why you sing for her and why it affects me." Alana swallows. "My mother died, too." Her hands touch the apron for reassurance. Will Morwen kill her for presuming that they have something in common?

"You're clever, for a human." Morwen adjusts her long white gown and sinks into a seat at a small table. It holds a platter with roasted meat. "Too bad you will probably die tomorrow."

Morwen puts her hand on the roasted creature and breaks off a leg with a popping sound. Then she inserts the joint into her mouth, twisting it counter-clockwise before pulling out the stripped bone. "Hungry?" She turns the platter in invitation.

Alana struggles to keep her face neutral as she stares at the roasted rabbit. Its charred head faces her.

She says, "We can both win."

Morwen tosses the bone onto the platter. "Tell me."

"We decide on an ingredient that would never be used in a cake. You'll choose the winner and I get to not die."

"Why would I help you?"

"Because," Alana says. She remembers the white hair clinging to Grace's curtain, a curtain swaying as if someone had leaped out to avoid discovery. "Rondo and Grace love each other. But you can't stand a relationship between Fey and mortal."

9

Alana doesn't say the rest: If mortals and Fey stopped feuding then Morwen would feel like her mother had died for no reason. Her brother's love is a betrayal of their mother.

Morwen pulls back her lips in a macabre smile that exposes her foxlike teeth. "You dare accuse my brother of loving a mortal?"

Alana keeps silent. The moon is full overhead. Were any villagers staring at it right now? Was her mother watching from above?

"There was no mention of recognizing ingredients." Morwen's green eyes gleam as she considers Alana's proposal. "Goblin fruit. You'll take a bite of it first. To prove your intention to stay."

Alana recoils. Yes, she wants to travel and see the world, but she wants the ability to go home to her village and her bakery, even to her careless father who didn't consider that if she won then she'd be indentured to the castle. "One bite means that I'm trapped here."

"You're not trapped. Our fruit opens your eyes to our magic. Humans don't want to leave after they can truly see." Morwen's expression turns cunning. "You wouldn't be leaving if you were Royal Baker."

"Ah." Alana nods as if this distinction is perfectly reasonable. "And how can I trust you? Give me your true name so that you do not eliminate me after I've won."

"My name?" Morwen grabs Alana's wrist and yanks her close, her other arm wrapping around. The rabbit grease makes Morwen's lips shiny. Her cruel eyes are irresistible. Alana wants to drown in those eyes, to float in a sea of green. She wants, oh God, she wants those lips to kiss her. She closes her eyes and Morwen's lips are firm, her tongue flicks. Alana's mouth opens. She wants more and moans, pressing against the Fey princess. She has never felt desire like this, an electricity in her veins.

"I'll kill you for the impudence," Morwen whispers into Alana's ear, but it sounds like a caress. Goosebumps run down Alana's arms. She doesn't want this moment to stop. Ever.

"You're magic," Alana says, forcing the words out. "Give me your name without telling me."

They stare at each other, still embracing, under the night sky and Alana has the feeling of the earth shifting under her feet, as if she cartwheels with the stars. She has never been alive before.

Then, Morwen releases her and Alana can breathe again.

"You first." Morwen reaches into the air overhead and presents a purple oval. "Eat."

Alana takes the Goblin fruit. It is soft and fits in the palm of her hand. "Name?"

When Morwen narrows her green eyes, Alana prompts, "Would you rather Grace wins?"

The princess makes a fist and then blows into it. When she opens her hand there is a necklace with a glass sphere containing flecks of gold. "Your turn."

This moment changes everything.

Alana bites into the Goblin fruit. Juice drips down her chin as she sucks at the pink fruit. She doesn't stop at one bite, she can't. The taste is sweet and tangy, refreshing and intoxicating. Dizzy, Alana drops the pit and reaches for the necklace, placing it around her neck and dropping the globe inside the collar of her dress. Alana stumbles back to the hallway, not because she can't see in the darkness—now she can—but because she is giddy from the fruit and sick about what she must do on the morrow.

In the morning, Alana paces as she talks herself through recipes. "Gold leaf. Dissolving chocolate bubble. Layers."

When someone knocks, Alana opens her door for Falcon, but has to blink. After eating the Goblin fruit, Alana can see the blue aura around Falcon's knife. And the minute berries entwined in the attendant's hair. As they walk outside, Alana laughs in joy. A centaur stands in the shade of the forest and magic sparks as the fish under the bridge flip around. She can almost understand the birds' chatter, like gossipy aunts. Alana kicks off her shoes to walk on velvet-grass. If she won Royal Baker, this perfect place would be home. Every night she could dine on Goblin fruit. Every day she would see Morwen to consult about meals and parties. The cruel princess is addictive and Alana wants more of her.

At her station, Alana names ingredients. This time when the air shimmers and there is a quick breeze, she sees the sprites that bring the ingredients and the way their wings flutter the air like hummingbirds. She feeds a log to the fire and laughs as the fire demon says, "Thank you, I was getting chilly" in a deep voice that she couldn't hear the day before.

She and Grace avoid each other, but Grace's knife strikes the cutting board and soon the smell of spices fills the air.

Alana slices the Goblin Fruit into tiny pieces. Her mouth waters, but she doesn't eat a piece. Instead, she concentrates on the chocolate shell. It must be perfect or it will melt too soon.

As the sun slides into position, the king, Princess Morwen, and Prince Rondo walk down the steps to the tent.

Falcon says, "Humans and Fey have arrived to watch the final judging."

Alana shakes her head. She has been concentrating so hard on the difficult baking that it takes her a heartbeat or two to realize.

"What?" she says. "Humans?"

"Yes, they arrived from your village," Morwen says in a bored tone. "They may watch from the ramparts."

Falcon bows and leaves to escort the audience to their place.

Two showpieces sit on the table: one a sphere of dark chocolate with gold leaf sprinkled like stars in a night sky. Or like Morwen's dark hair in a jeweled net. Next to it is a pitcher of warm Goblin fruit drizzle. The other cake is as bright as Alana's is dark: a three-layer chai, coffee, and Earl Grey cake with elaborate white fondant. Instead of yesterday's swan theme this is a dove. A bird to symbolize 'peace.'

Alana chews the inside of her cheek. As with the bread challenge, Grace has created a better entry. It is what Alana expected. Grace knew about this contest and had time to prepare. Alana remembers her father's palm in the center of her back, shoving her forward as he boasts.

The royal twins stare at the showpieces. A small smile hovers on Morwen's face. Rondo watches her with suspicion.

"Pleased with yourself?" he asks.

"Most pleased."

King Angus's eye twitches, but he remains standing.

Led by Falcon, the villagers stand high up on the wall that overlooks the baking tent. With the aid of the Goblin fruit, Alana sees village children pull at their mothers' hands as they point to the colorful fish in the streams. And, there is Papa. She recognizes his round body and the wisps of hair blowing in the wind. He waves frantically and Alana waves back.

"Win for us," he shouts.

He does not know she may end up a rabbit.

Falcon returns to the tent, shooting a disdainful look toward the ramparts. Alana understands the unspoken accusation. The villagers are dusty from travel and there is a collective stench of sheep and sweat and horse wafting on the wind. Alana wants to explain: these villagers aren't travelers, it was a big deal for them to come here, they want to be impressed.

"Serve the first cake," the king says.

Alana steps forward before Falcon can. She slices through the detailed dove decoration on the fondant of the chai cake. The inside is a beautiful color with specks of spice. She places a sample on three dainty plates.

Each judge takes a bite; Alana studies their faces.

"Each of the flavors comes through, the cake is moist, and the decoration is commendable. Nicely done," the king says, moving aside his plate. "Next."

Exhaling, Alana wipes her sweaty hands on her apron. This is it. She pours the warm Goblin fruit drizzle; the chocolate shell melts to reveal the inside.

The Fey hold inhumanly still. Alana becomes aware of her heartbeat, the shaking in her knees, the way her breath wheezes in and out.

"Is this a joke?" Rondo finally asks.

"You mayfly!" The Fey princess looks like she wants to rip the branches from her throne and stab them through Alana. Morwen leans across the table to whisper, "You will regret this."

"Maybe," Alana whisper back, "but you were never going to let me leave with your name. Once I realized that I had to improvise."

A necklace full of magic sits in a glob of melted chocolate.

"The first piece is for the princess," Alana says, willing her voice not to shake as she scoops the necklace onto a plate. She offers it to Morwen. "My gift to you."

Morwen lunges for the plate, but Alana holds it away.

"Do you accept my gift?" she asks, loudly and clearly.

"Cake was owed to me," Morwen says, looking around the tent for support. "This is no gift."

"This is not cake. This necklace was given to me and now I offer it back." Alana stares into the green eyes, though it takes a force of will. "As. A. Gift."

Yells drift down from the ramparts, questions about what is happening.

Falcon's hand drops to her knife. Fey from the forest emerge, creeping closer to the tent. The centaur has his bow drawn.

Rondo licks his lips, but King Angus says nothing.

Morwen glances to the villagers, to the Fey, to Falcon. Her eyes promise retribution, but she says, "I accept the gift" and takes the plate.

Alana knows this is not over.

"Vote," King Angus says.

"The chai," says Rondo, looking at Grace.

"As there was no second cake, I agree," says the king.

"And my vote makes it unanimous," Morwen says too sweetly. She smiles, radiant, as she calls out loud enough for all to hear, "Grace, you are now the Royal Baker."

Grace swivels her head toward Alana and then toward the judges, confused. "Thank you," she says. "I am honored."

Most in the audience of Fey and humans cheer, but Alana sees villagers shake their head in disappointment. Papa takes off his hat and holds it to his chest.

Grace turns to Alana. "What just happened?"

Under the cover of the cheering, Alana says, "I knew you would bake a better cake so I made a way for us both to survive."

"You gave a gift to earn a debt." Grace shakes her head. "All I was thinking about was cake."

"And love."

"You're from a small village." Grace dips her head so her red hair covers her blush. "I thought you would be disgusted."

"We need to understand each other." Alana looks at the Fey and mortals—not quite interacting. "This should be an annual competition. One in which losers aren't turned into rabbits."

Grace nods and moves toward Prince Rondo.

Suddenly, pointed fingernails are digging into Alana's neck. "You cheated," Morwen says, mouth close to Alana's ear, "And now you want to marry my father so you'll become queen and rule over us all."

Half-asleep, King Angus's eyes snap fully at that suggestion.

At the other end of the tent Prince Rondo and Grace are announcing an annual baking contest. Villagers cheer from the ramparts, Alana's defeat forgotten, and the centaur stomps his hooves. Even Falcon smiles.

"Fantastic idea, but no," Alana says. "Although marrying a member of the royal family could be the prize next year."

"Next year?" Morwen pulls back to stare at her brother and the audience's positive response to his announcement.

Alana swallows; the hand on her throat is so tight. "For my gift, I want to go home. Safely."

"You've eaten Goblin Fruit, you miserable mayfly," Morwen says, bringing her gaze back to Alana. She drops her hand. "Go ahead and leave. You'll wish you could return with every beat of your heart. Your village has lost all color, your food will have no taste. Happily, I agree to your request."

Alana wraps her hands in her apron. Morwen is right. She has changed and no one in the village will understand her pain. "Like you, I am the only daughter of my mother. I already live with a pain and loss that never ends because I cannot return to a world where she is alive. As a baker, though, I have learned the patience to wait for the dough to rise."

"Stupid mortal." Morwen thrusts the globe of the necklace into her mouth. Her sharp teeth break the glass. Her teeth crunch. Crimson blood flows from her mouth as the golden flecks of her name sink into her skin. "You didn't win." Bloody spittle hits Alana's face.

"No," Alana gives her a half-smile, "but maybe next year."

CHILD OF MOON AND SEA

*Suddenly a white wave rushed from the hole and scampered toward Elsa. She screamed.
As the ghost crabs advanced, Elsa retreated.*

Child of Moon and Sea

We never go swimming alone. Water swirled around Elsa Dalhquist's ankle and fed back into the next wavelet. It was hard to think, easier to feel. Her silken chemise nightgown fluttered against her skin; moonlit breeze brushed her shoulders. Weeks of insomnia muddied the mind. Elsa stepped forward into the surf, felt water between her thighs. A deep breath and then she dove into the ocean, the coldness surrounding her, the darkness complete.

She swam with no plan, no destination, just seeking physical exhaustion, a respite from circling thoughts. The rhythm of the waves was comforting, like being rocked by a giant hand. She went farther, her toned arms slicing through the saltwater. A feeling of alarm slowly made its way to her mind, but muffled, as if a little man was waving his cap and shouting from far away. Elsa ignored him. Perhaps drowning was not such a bad way to go. Stroke, stroke, stroke with your arms until you missed one, then two, and went down into the blackness of nothing. No more worries about her mentor's disapproval, about the whole department snickering when they saw her, no more wondering what to do without a research grant and it was already summer.

She missed a stroke. Water smacked Elsa in the face. She gasped, choked on the saltwater, the taste of it filled her mouth. With a strong kick Elsa turned to face the shore. Silence as she looked around, really looked, and found herself alone, in the dark, so far out that the strip of restaurants and houses between the piers looked like the lights you see from an airplane. She didn't have the strength to swim back.

Shaking as she realized exactly what she'd done, Elsa lit for shore, tried to settle into the crawl. If you die, she told herself, Dr. Buckston will think you drowned for unrequited love. Don't let him have the satisfaction. The headlines will be stupid: *Sleep-Therapist Dies After Ineffectual Struggles With Insomnia*, or *Recent Grad Sleep-Swims to Her Death. Part Of Her Thesis? Turn to Page 5.* It became harder to stay afloat. The illusion of being rocked by a giant hand evolved into a rag-doll Elsa, jerked about by an unseen puppeteer.

Closer now, the background resolved into outlines of beach houses. The pier, commercial center of Topsail Island, North Carolina, shimmered off to the right. Elsa's crawl had turned into a doggy-paddle. Every third wave or so washed over her and a stitch in her right side made her pant. Then her knees hit the sandbar, sand scratching flesh, and she struggled to stand up. Her sobs broke out to join tears. She didn't know how long she'd been crying, but she grabbed her sides and cried some more until it was over. Elsa splashed to shore, using the nighttime lights of the community pool as a focal point because the current had pulled her south.

Calves pinging from trudging in the sand, she made her way toward her penthouse suite in the house she was sharing with her brother's family. William and his wife Kelly had the master suite on the main floor. Their three children occupied the second-floor bedrooms. A house full of people, but Elsa alone in her king-sized bed. She'd fantasized about inviting Grady, Dr. Buckson. That, of course, couldn't happen now. Not after she'd told him about her crush and he'd given a little laugh and patted her arm. Humiliating, but not as bad as losing the grant she'd been expecting to continue working in the sleep lab next year for post-doc work. Elsa shook her head. *I almost drowned to get rid of these thoughts, and here they are, waiting for me on the shore.*

Off to the side, thin tape fluttered in the breeze, a sign that nesting turtles needed protection. She became aware of sand shifting near her feet and looked down at several ghost crabs. Little creatures, translucent to white, barely visible in the dark. Their black eyes balanced on stalks. Elsa shivered. Little alien faces. The crabs popped out of their holes and scuttled toward the ocean. Children loved to chase them, but Elsa viewed them as albino spiders.

Distracted by the crabs, Elsa almost missed the turn-off to the beach house. She turned back to look at the ocean. She could have died. No one would have known. The transient glow of false dawn created a shadow out on the sandbar where she'd been earlier. Her eyes narrowed. A man stood there, tall, wet hair plastered back, chest bare and longboard shorts riding low on lean hips. Dark eyes over a thin mustache and a goatee shaped to form an upside down letter 'T.' A surfer, she thought. Despite the physical distance between them, Elsa felt an instant connection with this stranger, the only two beings conscious at this moment of pre-dawn day.

She hurried up the outside steps to her penthouse suite.

Later that morning Elsa checked her outfit in the mirror: swimsuit, beach cover-up, and sunglasses. Without benefit of the moon's luminosity, her pale skin looked washed out. She sighed and, canvas chair in hand, went down to the beach.

Her brother William set up a cabana while his wife Kelly stood with one hand on her hip, the other shading her eyes as she kept watch over their children.

"Nice of you to join us," William grunted from where he was burying the cabana legs. After a final pat, he stood, brushing sand off his hands. Like Elsa, William was tall and fair with understated features they'd inherited from their Swedish mother. He had an athletic build, strong hands, and a good-paying job. A Viking with a laptop.

"Sorry I missed breakfast. I slept in."

"You look like you could use more sleep. There are circles under your eyes."

"Being away from Baltimore should help. A couple nights of quality sleep and I'll take on the world." Elsa looked out at the water, anticipating uncomfortable questions about graduate school, career plans, and whether she was dating anyone.

He continued assembling the cabana. "Sleep is important," William said. "I remember when Kelly breastfed and was up several times a night. She went crazy."

"I heard my name. What are you talking about?"

William placed a sunburned arm around his wife. "Sleep deprivation."

Kelly pushed Gucci sunglasses atop her highlighted hair. "You have trouble sleeping?"

"Sometimes," Elsa said. *Don't be defensive*, she told herself.

"With three kids, someone is always sick, needs consoling after a bad dream, or has to go to the bathroom," Kelly said. "If I were single I would sleep like the dead every night." She opened the cooler, handed William a bottled water then offered one to Elsa, who declined.

"Insomnia is hardly a choice," Elsa said with annoyance. She wondered, not for the first time, what William saw in Kelly.

"Why don't you do something productive with the time?" Kelly asked. Kelly dug in the cooler for a bottle of milk. "When I can't sleep I catch up on my reading or marinate chicken breasts for dinner. Time is a gift, if you use it wisely."

Elsa swallowed. "It's forced overstimulation. Think *A Clockwork Orange* with your eyelids propped open."

"Someone's a little sensitive," Kelly said.

William interrupted. "Hey, look at Dylan. He's doing great on that boogie board."

Kelly frowned at her husband. She diverted her attention to Abby, instead, playing with colorful plastic beach toys nearby.

Elsa felt grateful, and a little surprised, that her brother had intervened. "Where's Caitlyn?"

"Over there." Kelly pointed to a patch at the water's edge. Elsa walked toward her niece.

"Auntie Elsa!" Caitlyn grinned, revealing a missing tooth. "I didn't know if you were coming. Will you help me look for shark's teeth?"

"I would never miss a chance to do that with you." They wandered over the wet sand, sifting through shells and pebbles.

"I wasn't sure. Daddy said you were on a different schedule because your job was to watch people sleep. That's so weird."

Elsa wrinkled her nose, tried to explain. "To help people with sleep problems, I have to know what's going on while they are sleeping."

Caitlyn appeared to have lost interest. "How come you went right up to your room when you got here? I wanted to see you, but Daddy said not to disturb you. Are you sick?"

"No, honey. I'm fine." Elsa crouched near her niece and raked the sand with her fingers. "I got stuck in traffic at the drawbridge. I was very tired."

"Mommy said you need a man."

Elsa ignored the comment. "Look what I found." Elsa balanced a tiny black triangle on her fingertip. "First shark tooth of the vacation."

That night Elsa waited until the lights in the beach house went off before slipping on a two-piece. She went out the balcony door and tiptoed down the stairs, hoping to see the mystery man. They had a connection, she felt, two beings who eschewed the mundane, yearned for something more spiritual, something primal found in the water, in the transition from night to day, acting out the subconscious. Someone who understood her.

It took her a few minutes to find the lone swimmer and when she did the tips of her ears burned. Elsa took off her wrap and tied it around the leg of William's darkened cabana so it wouldn't blow away. While feeling a bit self-conscious in the bikini, she also hoped the man would turn around and admire her body. She imagined telling him, "This is how women from Sweden are meant to be viewed—in the moonlight. We are children of the moon and sea."

The ocean embraced her. Elsa swam toward the man, careful to maintain some distance. She felt a thrill, wondering if he had gone swimming again to attract her attention. Perhaps he wanted to be alone with her.

You're romanticizing again, she acknowledged.

The man was taller than her, broader. Where Dr. Buckston impersonated a lion, this man was silent, a real predator. Standing on a sandbar, she guessed, only the top half of his body visible. His eyes were dark, as if all pupil, his skin tight, almost gray in the moonlight. His chest muscular and hairless. Elsa wondered if he shaved for vanity. Above the water she saw thick forearms with articulated fingers ending in blunt fingernails. Tools, she thought. His body is designed for purpose.

Elsa relaxed into the rhythm of the dark water's push and pull. From the corner of her eye she saw fins approaching. Fear ran from her belly to her throat. One triangle submerged, another surfaced. She couldn't be sure whether she was seeing two or ten beasts. Elsa looked around for the man. He had vanished.

You broke the rule: you swam alone. Elsa rode to shore on the next wave and tried to remember the difference between dolphins and sharks. Don't look over your shoulder. Forward motion to survive. Her foot scraped bottom and she scrambled out of the water. Running to William's cabana, she collapsed, gasping, onto a chaise.

When she'd caught her breath she strained to see the fins—and the man. All were invisible. She told herself that he must have left the water before the sharks arrived. She'd have seen a frenzy if there'd been an attack. Feeling calmer, Elsa stood and gazed at the quiet water.

The next morning Elsa joined William's family at the beach, feeling as if she were stepping into required vacation routine. Dylan and Caitlyn played Frisbee while Kelly rummaged through a beach bag and eighteen-month-old Abby sat in an inflatable pool in the shade of the cabana. William sprawled in a beach chair with his iPhone.

"Hey Elsa," Kelly said, "Would you watch the kids while I pick up some things for Friday's dinner?"

"Sure." Elsa sat beside the pool and made gentle waves for the toddler with her hand. Abby cooed.

"Last night I saw fins in the water. I don't know if they belonged to dolphins or sharks."

William looked up. "What time? Dolphins usually swim by at dawn and dusk."

"It was in the middle of the night. I saw them from my balcony, right in front of our house."

"A dolphin's dorsal fin is rounded at the top; a shark's is straight. Sharks swim back and forth. Dolphins swim up and down." He gestured to illustrate the difference.

22

He played with the iPhone again. "So which was it?"

Elsa shrugged. "Too far away to tell." She smiled at Abby, but watched William out of the corner of her eye. "I thought there was a man out there too."

William grinned. "Literally swimming with the sharks? I hope not."

Elsa didn't answer.

"Are you afraid of the water now?" he asked.

"Me? Too scared to go swimming? I'm a first-generation Swede." She smiled back at her brother. "We grew up hearing mom's stories about Odin and Loki. Thor wrestling sea-serpents."

"And brave chieftains dying heroic deaths. That's key."

"Morbid!"

"No," William said. "That's how you became a demigod yourself. Or, at least, you became a totem or nature spirit."

"That's right." Elsa pulled Abby out of the pool and onto her lap. "I'd forgotten that part."

"There's a reason for these myths. The ocean is a different world, about ninety percent of which you can't see." William shrugged. "Fins aside, you may want to get your swimming in now."

"Why's that?"

"The Weather Channel says we're in for some rough weather from the hurricane forming near Florida. It's going to be moving up the coast later in the week. I hope we won't have to evacuate."

"Maybe it'll shift course."

He shook his head. "Unlikely."

Throughout the rest of the day Elsa imagined that the man from the ocean was somewhere nearby. He would have to be staying around here, she reasoned, why else would he be swimming in front of our rental? He'll swim again tonight, she hoped. She went up to her room early, longing to get through the day the way she used to try getting through the night.

That night on her balcony, it took less than a minute to pick out the man swimming past the breakers. She ran down the steps and swam to meet him, determined to find out more. Her arms cut through the water and the man turned to watch, as if waiting for her. His face was luminous and, in the sepia light from the waning moon, flawless. When she was close enough to see his eyes, black and flat, she said, "I looked for you on the beach, yesterday and today."

He said nothing. His hand, colder than the water, reached for hers. Under the salt scent of the ocean Elsa smelled something like vinegar. Or urine. Together they rode a high wave, Elsa's feet kicked through the water, but she couldn't touch bottom. Her heart beat with excitement. She laughed. Together they climbed each wave, his hand still holding hers. She squeezed tightly and felt gratified when he did not pull away.

The next wave pushed Elsa under. His strong arms raised her above the breakers. Water washed over the man's face, but he didn't seem to mind. He lowered her against his body. Together they treaded water to stay afloat, her arms around his neck. Elsa closed her eyes when he leaned in to kiss her.

You are kissing a stranger in dangerous conditions, an inner voice warned.

The chilly water swirled around them. He held her face, his lips pressing against hers. Heat flushed her body. His hand moved to her back and Elsa felt the pressure on her bare skin. The kiss ended. She opened her eyes. In place of his obsidian eyes she gazed at eye sockets of oyster shells. Had the moonlight done magic? It appeared that his features had melted, becoming ill-defined. The spray made it difficult to see in the dying moonlight. He pulled Elsa closer, both hands on her back. Something wound itself around her legs. "Oh my God, there's something in the water!"

Panic. Elsa kicked her feet to no avail. The man leaned in as if to kiss her again. His hand felt like sandpaper pulling her closer. Elsa pushed away, but he wouldn't release her. "Let me go." She wiggled in his arms, desperate, then propelled herself into the on-coming wave. Adrenaline pumping, she was no match for the force of the wall of water.

Elsa went under. Thunder filled her ears and grit scratched her flesh. When she opened her eyes, all was watery-black. Her hand touched sand. In an attempt to brace against the bottom, Elsa extended her legs, but the water swirled her around like a sock in a washing machine. Her chest ached for oxygen.

I could die and no one would know.

She felt hands on her, pulling her up and out of harm's way. Elsa opened her eyes, gasping for breath. He looped an arm under her legs, supported her back, and carried her tight against his cold, smooth chest until they were in waist-high water where he released her. She stumbled to shore, glanced over her shoulder.

Was he trying to kill me or save me?

Fingers of wind from every direction. Elsa coughed, saltwater burning her eyes and throat. William's storm had arrived, buffeting Topsail.

Wind buffeting the walls woke her. She was stiff from sleeping on the floor where she'd collapsed. The bedspread covered her exhausted body. The bedside clock read 7:43. Unsure if that meant 7 'A.M' or 'P.M,' Elsa looked outside for context. The storm raged, framed in picture windows meant to showcase sunshine.

Elsa showered. The warm water washed away the sand and grit and soothed her sore muscles. Images from last night played in her mind.

She rubbed where the seaweed had tangled around her calves. No marks on her legs. She saw the man's black eyes and then oyster shells where his eyes should have been. But that didn't make sense. It made more sense that she'd projected her fear onto the man. *I almost died and he saved me.* She should be more worried about her romantic brazenness with the stranger.

Elsa toweled off and chose khaki shorts and a hoodie. She was pleased with her image in the mirror: sparkling eyes, skin lightly bronzed. Would the man recognize her in the daylight? She wondered what he was doing right now.

She left her room and was making her way down the stairs when she heard her name.

"I don't understand why Elsa sleeps all the time."

"Kelly, she's depressed about something."

"She needs some structure; to get up early in the morning and go to bed at a reasonable hour—like the rest of the world. We're halfway through the vacation and she's missing it."

Elsa pictured Kelly standing there with hands on hips and a constipated expression on her face.

"Sweetie, I know you want to help. I think I've told you, Elsa had night terrors as a kid. Mom had them too."

I'm not crazy, Elsa thought as she closed her eyes against a feeling of shame. *I just need a small victory.*

"I get it, William. Nightmares are scary. Everyone has them…"

"Night terrors are different. It's a medical condition that can be triggered by stress, medications, being overtired. Elsa internalizes stuff and it all comes out when she's asleep. If we pressure her, the internalized stress will develop into night terrors."

"Fine. I just think…"

The stair creaked. Elsa hoped they hadn't heard her. She continued down the stairs and rounded the corner to the kitchen into a domestic tableau where she was the only oddity. Kelly whisked eggs near the sink while at the table William hid behind his laptop. A game of Uno cards spread out before Dylan and Caitlyn, and Abby threw Cheerios from a high chair.

"Do you think the storm will end soon?" Elsa asked her brother.

He kept on working. "Afraid not. It's just starting. We'll have a break this afternoon and get pounded again tonight."

"I'm making scrambled eggs. Do you want some?" Kelly asked.

"Sure," Elsa said. Feeling antsy, she walked to the window and peered out.

"You're pacing like a cat," William said. He continued to peck at the keyboard.

"Am I bothering you?" Elsa asked.

"A little bit. I'm trying to concentrate, and I'm wondering what's so fascinating out there. I see rain."

Elsa shook her head. "There's nothing to see."

She stomped up the stairs to her room and sank into a wicker chair. She took out her phone, flipped it open, and shut it. While slipping the phone into her purse, she touched something that rattled. She pulled out her sleeping pills. She hadn't needed a pill at bedtime since she'd taken up night swimming. Now she needed sleep, not thinking time. She withdrew one white capsule. Then another. She tossed them into her mouth and chased them with bottled water.

She was being watched, she could feel it. Elsa got out of bed and went to the sliding glass door. A dark shadow stood outside. She pulled back the gauzy curtain. Lightning flashed. The man stood outside, dark hair dripping over a grayish face, chest bare, his oyster eyes a macabre mask. "Let me in." Elsa's hand went to the lock, then hesitated.

A few minutes later, she was in bed, Grady beside her. His blond hair was rumpled. He smiled and said, "No. Never."

Water rushed under the door, poured through the windows, and swept Grady away. He vanished, his mouth forming an 'O' of alarm. Elsa floated on her back in the cold water. Beneath her swam sea creatures. The man rose up from the brackish water. He walked toward Elsa with no fear. Then his arms encircled Elsa. Seaweed tangled in her hair. Fish swam by, bumping her. All the while the man held her.

"Who are you?" she asked.

Looking into her eyes, he said, "Tursas."

"Why are you here?"

"You came to me because you wanted to die." He smiled and his mouth split open into rows of triangular teeth.

Elsa struggled to wake up, half-conscious, as an orgasm rippled through her. Her hips rocked and she moaned through open lips. Her eyes fluttered open and she sat up, looking around the empty room. She felt disoriented, guilty. And still aroused.

Sliding back down, she listened to the rain, felt her heart slowing. *We never go swimming alone.*

Tursas. The name from the dream. He was a character from the stories her mother told when she and William were children. He was a boogeyman, a sea monster, revealing himself if they broke the rule.

Before dawn she returned to the first dream. Tursas stood at her door in the pouring rain, his eyes black with thick lashes, naked, his hands splayed across the glass so that the webbing between his fingers was exposed. "Live or die?" he said. "You called yourself a child of the moon and sea." Elsa sat in her large white bed, in a room of white furniture and white walls. The man's image grew dimmer as the sun rose behind him.

The next morning, Thursday, the lack of wind was startling after two days of the house shaking. Elsa dressed and went to the beach. A crowd had gathered near the water's edge. Excited voices filled the air. William tried to put the cabana back together. Kelly sat nearby, holding Abby.

"What's going on?" Elsa asked

Kelly shivered. "It's revolting. I should call Dylan and Caitlyn away."

Elsa watched as more people approached. Her niece and nephew had pushed through the throng.

"It's nature," William said. He shoved a pole into position.

"No," said Kelly. "Watching a shark swim around the aquarium is nature. This is voyeuristic. I feel bad for the animal. He's a spectacle."

Elsa's legs felt wobbly. Haltingly, she walked toward the water's edge. She pressed forward to join her niece and nephew and looked down at a dead shark, its nose pointed straight at Elsa's window. The water lapped at its tail. As the water came up to the shark's underbelly and retreated, it took the creature's intestines with it. Elsa sucked in her breath.

"Must have been hurt in that storm last night," said a sunburned man in a pink shirt. Elsa recognized him as a neighbor.

"But why would it come onshore?" A woman asked.

The sunburned man shrugged. "Probably got turned around."

"Do you think it was attacked? What made that hole in its side?"

"Hard to say."

"I'm surprised other sharks didn't have a feeding frenzy, rip him to pieces." People knelt for pictures by the carcass. Some flexed their arms to show their biceps as if they were responsible for landing the shark.

Elsa stifled the urge to scream. She put her hands on Dylan and Caitlyn's shoulders. "Leave him alone," she whispered. She shepherded the children toward the shade of the cabana. The children launched a kite while William, Kelly, and Elsa watched the group surrounding the shark.

"I don't want the children to go swimming today. Dylan will be disappointed, but I'm putting away the boogie board." Kelly stood up and shook out her beach towel.

William tipped his head. "An anomaly from the storm. Sharks don't come in past the breakers."

"Still," Kelly said. "We'll let the ocean calm down."

The man in the pink shirt walked to the cabana. He rested his hands on the frame and peered under the rim.

"A fellow called animal control. They aren't concerned so we're thinking about burying it before it starts to rot and smell up the whole beach. You guys got some shovels?"

William stared at the man and then looked away. "There's two right there." He gestured to the children's sand shovels.

The man set his mouth and walked next door.

Elsa couldn't get rid of the image of ropy intestines trailing from the carcass. Caitlyn pulled on Elsa's arm. "Why don't they just put him back? That's what we do when we dig up clams."

That shark is pointing right at my window. Like a message, but I don't know what it means.

"I guess they got their posse together," William commented.

Four men broke through the circle of gawkers and grabbed the shark's fins and tail. Like pallbearers they proceeded past William's cabana to the sand hill between the beach houses.

The men dug a shallow hole and tossed in the shark, covering it with sand.

Kelly signaled the children. "Put the kite away. I'm taking you to play miniature golf. It's too depressing around here."

Elsa sat on her room's deck, hugging her knees. The moon was shrinking, waxing gibbous, she thought. William would know the proper term. She felt the restlessness of insomnia coming on—that feeling where the mind circles and can't move forward. She'd lost track of time. Going down the outside steps, she glanced at her brother's window. Dark. She entered the water with a shiver. Half-heartedly playing in the surf, she felt fearful, but her need to see the man, to see why she confused him with a story from her childhood, overrode her anxiety. She dipped her toes in the water, several degrees colder than she remembered. She took a few steps back and rubbed her arms while surveying the beach. A bonfire blazed in the direction of the pier. "He's waiting for his own friends to go to bed before he can come meet me," she whispered, but she didn't believe it.

Elsa gazed at the mound between the beach houses and shivered. She walked to the wooden steps and sat on the bottom one. Tears of frustration flowed. She remembered the man kissing her in the water, his hand raising her up when she was drowning. *What is the connection between this man and Tursas?* She fell asleep leaning against a wooden railing.

She awoke with a stiff neck. The sky had turned grey and pink, a flat orange line stretched across the horizon. She looked for some sign that he'd come: a note, a footprint, maybe a blanket to cover her. *You're creating a one-sided romance, Elsa,* she chided herself. *Just like you did with Dr. Grady Buckston.* Thrusting her chilled hands in her pockets, she stood. Her right index finger touched the black shark's tooth she'd found with Caitlyn.

A seagull cried and pelicans flew silently overhead as she climbed the stairs to her room.

Friday dinner at the beach was traditionally a Swedish feast for the Dahlquist family before leaving the next morning. William worked in the kitchen to make Toast Skagen with shrimp and roe, beef patties with capers and pickled beets, while Kelly set out the pickled herring, lingonberry jam and blueberry soup she'd brought down. The adults finished with a shot of vodka. William went out to the deck and Elsa followed, looking over her shoulder into the house to see if Kelly was coming. Kelly stood at the counter to down a second shot before grabbing her glass of wine. "Last night of vacation." She winked at Elsa as she walked outside. One hand reached out for support against the doorframe. Elsa looked away, uncomfortable, and adjusted her chair for a better view of the ocean.

Wind blew over the three adults creating a backsplash of noise.

"So you'll be heading back up to Baltimore tomorrow?" William said.

Elsa didn't want to answer, but forced herself, "Actually, I don't think so."

"What?" William's expression wavered between anger and confusion. "Aren't you still working with that sleep therapist?"

Pain and disappointment clutched Elsa's insides. "He's a cognitive behavioral therapist for insomnia."

"What does that mean?" Kelly said.

William growled at her. "It means a guy who teaches you how to sleep. What happened? You were always talking about how great he was."

Tears threatened and Elsa turned away. "My grant wasn't renewed for next year. I thought it would be so I didn't apply anywhere else."

Kelly leaned over. "But you already have your degree."

William said, "You co-authored a study with that guy! Why didn't he make sure you got the grant?"

Elsa looked down into her folded hands. That was the question that tortured her. She'd more than respected Dr. Grady Buckston. She'd idolized him. And then, one night while they were working together in the lab she'd done the unthinkable. She'd told him in stumbling awkward words how she felt. And then her fellowship went to someone else. Stupid, stupid, stupid.

"I don't know," she said to William. "There are a lot of qualified people vying for research money. Guess it was someone else's turn."

"So what are you going to do, Elsa?" William folded his arms across his chest.

"Come on William, she's young, she's pretty, she's got a degree. The world is her oyster." Kelly threw out her arms in grand gesture. The wine glass balanced on the end of her chair fell to the deck and broke. William went inside, slamming the sliding door behind him.

Kelly laughed.

Anger burned away Elsa's self-pity. It felt good. "What's so funny you... you tits-on-a-stick?"

"Sink or swim, babe." Kelly pushed herself out of the wooden lounge chair. "Bartend, answer phones, get a pay check and a new place to live. If you're not moving forward, you're dying."

Kelly shoved her face into Elsa's and enunciated with a drunk's over-precision, "Sink or fucking swim." She laughed again as she went inside, leaving Elsa alone with the broken glass.

4:55 a.m. Bags packed. Staring at the ceiling, same position as the first night of this week. Images of the dead shark interspersed with circular thoughts about finding a job, not returning to Baltimore, researching other grants to study insomnia. Impatience building up, as if she should be doing something. *Sink or swim.* A quick tapping sound followed by raindrops spotting the window. Two steps and she was there, looking for his wet-dark head, his muscled chest, his mouth forming the words, live or die.

Compelled by the image, Elsa went down the wooden steps in the limited light of a cloud-shadowed moon. Not long till sunrise. Rain continued to fall. She grabbed her niece's pink-handled shovel from where it leaned against the wooden step and floundered toward the burial mound. She knelt and thrust the shovel into the sand and began to dig. The shovel broke. She tossed aside the handle and, grabbing the shovel head, dug anew. Sand flew. Fear grew inside Elsa, but she had to keep going. Smell, putrid, emanated with physical force. Elsa gagged, leaning back and breathing through her mouth until the breeze dissipated the main stench.

One more thrust and she exposed the animal, laying on its side. Gray body, gills, black pupils, an apex predator. Landlocked, no way to move forward, to swim away. Like her. Suddenly a white wave rushed from the hole and scampered toward Elsa. She screamed. As the ghost crabs advanced, Elsa retreated. She tripped on the hem of her nightgown and fell backwards. Crabs spewed from the hole, paraded over the skirt of her gown.

Elsa cried out, hands batting the nightgown until the procession had passed. Shivering, she crept forward, her gown clinging to her chilled body.

"Tursas." She reached into the hole and caressed the shark's skin from head to tail so that it felt smooth under her fingers. "I want to live, even with failure."

32

Elsa stood and heaved the heavy corpse from its shallow grave. It had taken four men to carry it before and now she was by herself. *I don't think I can do this.* Dragging it by the fin toward the water, her grip loosened and the shark skin—abrasive sandpaper when rubbed backwards from tail to head—penetrated her flesh, drawing blood. Sacrifice. *You called the shark-man, now you pay.*

Wrapping her arms around the body, she struggled to the water, the shark stench filling her nose. Waves pulled at the body, but Elsa held on, ignoring the pain, the shrieking of her muscles until they were past the sandbar. She released the shark with a splash. The ocean surged as if wrapping watery arms around the shark. She watched the beast drift away until it blurred with the water, then rubbed her aching arms. Her toes stretched into the sand and she let her palms rest on the surface, open to a profound awareness of the ocean's inhabitants. She knew the clams below the surface, the loggerhead turtles, the fish swimming by, and other sea creatures she could not name. Dawn bloomed: an ethereal mix of sunlight and rain. Fishing boats spread across the horizon line.

Breakage

*W*e remember that Myra and her daughter, Little Jessica, were the first to Break. Myra moved into our neighborhood pregnant, her belly swollen and her face glowing. The couple loved the paved sidewalks and road signs that cautioned *Slow! Kids at play.* They would be safe here, they thought. Then, after Jessica had been born and grown into an adorable pony-tailed preschooler, she pulled on her mother's arm and demanded a second ice pop in a whiny tone. Myra was standing outside talking to another neighbor. Myra grasped Jessica's forearm—everyone agreed that it was no firmer than normal—and gave her a little shake. "You need to wait until the adults have finished speaking before you interrupt."

Little Jessica dissolved into tears and sank down to the sidewalk. Her mother grew from angry to alarmed as the violence of the sobs increased. With an apologetic look at the neighbor, Myra sank down and touched Jessica on the forearm. "I didn't hurt you, Jessica. I just wanted you to wait a moment."

Myra pulled up the preschooler's long sleeve and the material snagged at a certain section. Tugging harder, Myra gasped. Jessica's arm had broken clean through, the section from forearm to finger-tips gone solid as a store's mannequin. No blood or broken flesh.

Jessica's stump was jagged, hard as plastic. The stump's edges had caught the sleeve.

❧

Today, right now, my husband says, "Why don't you want to go to my mother's house for the holiday?" He emphasizes the word "don't" instead of "why" and I understand this to be an argument rather than a conversation. Already I am exhausted. Not by the fight, but from biting my tongue. Anger grinds in my throat and I swallow, imagining little bits of my esophagus flaking away, falling into my stomach, and floating in a sea of gastric acid.

❧

Danny was our second neighbor to Break. An adult. No one touched him. He was the kind to push down his anger, chew on it for breakfast, lunch, and dinner. Then, he'd explode and we'd hear him yelling from a couple houses away. He was always sorry, embarrassed afterwards. His family was embarrassed too, but he never hit them or anything. The damage was to himself.

And so it was. We heard the yelling and came outside. Danny stumbled from his house, his neck straining, his face red. He looked like that old TV show *The Hulk*, but this wasn't special effects and it sure wasn't funny. His hands were around his throat as he struggled to breathe. His chest heaved and we saw it expanding, his shirt stretched to the point of buttons popping off. It was a race between his red face and his exploding chest and then both burst. Bits of plastic flew outward from the force. We shooed the kids inside, of course. His body buckled at the knees and fell, headless, to the sidewalk. Like Little Jessica, the chest turned to mannequin plastic, the neck sealed off, too. We remember how, after, the parts we picked up were still warm with his breath.

More cracks appeared after that. Two fingers missing from a hand, a pair of jeans stapled below the knee, an eye turned plastic that only looked forward. Our Breakage was visible, scars on view to each other. We found a kind of freedom, a raw honesty, in this

36

inability to hide our pain. Our community became close; no one moved in and no one moved out.

I say to my husband, "It's not fair to the kids. Traveling four hours in the car to spend two hours visiting. I'd rather stay here and work in the garden, maybe use the grill. Things we don't have time to do during the week."

"We're going," he says as if it were decided. He's not like me, like us. Instead, he's so confident in his ability to shape and push what he wants that he doesn't feel the helpless anger that Breaks us. He sees the physical manifestation of our pain as a weakness.

My daughter stands in the doorway. I don't know how long she's been listening.

I drop my eyes to half-mast so I don't have to see him, to see any victory on his face, or worse, dispassion. I give a nod, acquiescing before there is more Breakage, but as I do I hear the static of minute fractures like ice on a pond. Instinctually, I tighten my body to hold it together, afraid to release and find Breakage in my neck or maybe in my shoulders this time. It is not enough to speak agreement, but swallow frustration and hurt. I need to keep talking.

Last week it was two teenagers. Mixing hormones and drama makes Breakage inevitable, but still devastating. Jimmy Warcol, who used to knock on our doors prepared to mow in summer and shovel in winter, fell in love with Carrie Ann from the cul-de-sac. She was pretty with long hair and those strong legs from play-ing varsity soccer. We saw the Breaks when they stopped dating, both hurt. We thought he needed more sympathy because he had trouble breathing after. Our guesses were his lungs had cracked or maybe some words had gotten trapped in his throat and caused a plastic blockage, the tissue no longer sliding as it should. But then he started dating another girl and the next day Carrie Ann was dead. A broken heart is what we agreed on, but some said it was the jealousy of being replaced. Whatever it was, Carrie Ann's heart fractured. Her mother said she could feel pieces hard as a stone when she tried to revive her dead daughter.

After Jimmy heard the news, he crawled into his closet, shut the door, and curled into a ball. His family found him there, his body entirely turned to plastic, forever in fetal position.

⚵

"I don't want to go." I unspool the words like a necklace of pearls.

"Then stay here." He shrugs. I can tell he thought we'd finished the conversation. "I'll take the kids."

It feels like a threat of abandonment. "I don't want to be left behind." I try to find the true words underneath the fear that tells me to lash out. "I want to enjoy the holiday with my family, in my own house, with no pressure."

"It's okay, we can go." My daughter wants to make peace. She understands.

"Make your choice."

My hands clench and my jaw is so tight that my head aches. These emotions that make us vulnerable, that make us whisper when we argue, are the flip side of the love we can feel. All the parts make us human.

I bite my tongue and feel my teeth sink down. I open my mouth to answer and a small piece of pink falls out. My cheeks flush with anger as I pick it up. The tip of my tongue turned to plastic. I open my mouth and run my finger across the new edge, trying to remember which taste buds are on the tongue tip.

My Own Skin

It doesn't hurt to peel off our outer layer—*pelli*—but tonight when we do, we are nervous. They pronounce our skin "pelts" and call us "selkies," something from their home world. That was one of the original misunderstandings when they came from the stars to our home. That is not what we call ourselves. And our *pelli* is more than skin, more than a shell, more than fur, it is the part that connects our emotions and thoughts to our physical form.

Tonight, we come ashore together, threading through the black rocks that jut like teeth in a ring that encloses this island. Then, we take off our *pellis*. Two moons light the beach in a soft pink glow. Big Sister pulls at the tides, regular and uniform. Little Sister is the troublemaker. Her skin is pockmarked with volcanoes, her crown is a red corona in the sky. Her flight path is erratic: when she is angry, she yanks at us, causing peaks in our oceans, and eroding shorelines.

We are a pod, so we act together. We set our *pellis* on the black sand in little piles, some transparent and some taking on a soft gray hue as if to match the sand. Tonight we do not want to let go of it, but we are resolved. One of us is missing and we will get them back. We choose a form—some like the newcomer females and some like the males and some with attributes of both or neither. This is funny to us because with our *pelli* we take whatever form we want whenever we want.

This isn't the first time we have shifted so we know how to wiggle our fingers and toes. Some have already begun the dance. It is so different on land than in the sea. Gravity makes us teeter as we stretch away from the sand, arms extended for balance, and then fall to the forgiving beach. And when one comes over to help another up, perhaps they become a tangle of limbs.

The feel of wind is so different than water, but dancing keeps us warm. We know the pattern and soon we flow. And as we create harmony, as we are together, so does our bliss grow. In our *pellis*, our thoughts are open to the pod. By taking them off, we separate and open ourselves to a new way to create beauty through movement.

We sense the newcomer. Awareness passes among us, a resolve, and we hold tight to the dance's form until tension breaks us. We scatter. Grab for our individual *pellis* so we can change form and dive into the friendly water, hide behind the rocky teeth that dash the newcomers' boats.

The newcomer, alone, steps from behind the dune where they'd been hiding, form enveloped in a giant hooded coat. They are done watching our dance. Now their legs pump as they run toward the beach.

We all get away but one.

There is a breaking inside, a ripping as if a leviathan from the deep had bitten us, taken one away, leaving wounds inside of the survivors. Water splashes against the rocks.

We are gone.

No.

They are gone.

I am here.

The newcomer is shoving my *pelli* into a sack and I cannot move. I am a woman, now, and this body feels strange. I reach for my pod with my mind, but there is an absence. I am trying to wave an appendage that doesn't exist in this form. My breath quickens, my torso expands and I am afraid. I have never been separated from my pod and this body does not talk to me. A moment ago, there was harmony in our dance, but now this newcomer has stolen

40

from me. My mind, this woman's mind, knows words, but I don't have the concept.

I try, "Please?"

"You must be cold," he says. How do I know it is a he? This body knows.

I touch my head. Hair grows there, and under my armpits, and where my legs come together, but nowhere else to keep me warm. I shiver.

He is not ungentle as he wraps me in a blanket, my arms held down by my sides, and then scoops me up, carrying me up to the buildings the newcomers built. Alone in my mind, I repeat that this was the plan. That one of us had to be captured. We made the decision and I must carry it out. Over his shoulder I see the moon sisters. Red streams down Little Sister's face and makes me think of tears. I know what tears are now. This body has taught me.

We took their form because we could and they couldn't take ours. We took their form because this is a planet of water and they do not have the right bodies for it. We took their form because we felt sorry that these newcomers had no fur for the cold.

But we did not misunderstand when they stole our *pellis*—and our people—like the leviathans from the deep. Leviathans do not mask their intent. Their jaws open wide and their breath smells of death. They—the newcomers—came with mouths full of teeth, but they hid them behind smiles.

Inside the building, he sets me down and puts something over my head that covers my body. Clothing. Table. Light. The words rush at me. We've—no, I've—experienced this expedited learning when changing forms before, but this human body is complicated.

The table is too large for the two of us; it is solid and made for many people. We do not have this thing under the seas. His metal lantern casts a ring of light and shadow, but my lanterns, the sister moons, hang in the sky. I can see them from the windows behind this man: Big Sister edging out of sight, Little Sister moving into frame. I feel the sea creep up the island in push-pull increments and imagine the sound increasing as water slaps at the black rock teeth.

"You'll live with us now. It will take some time, but you'll get used to it here." He speaks with such authority that each statement

41

traps me in this human body; my bare skin hurts. "This will be a good life for you."

"I do not belong here." I lift the dress that he put over my head and slap at my legs. The fabric is coarse and I long for my sleek skin and warm fur.

"They call me Flicks." He leans forward. "What's your name?"

What do I call myself? I don't know how to answer this so I shrug my shoulders.

"We can help each other. Your pelt-sy," he mangles the word, "is the most amazing bio-aril we've ever seen. The lab is trying to figure it out. They think maybe a gel that holds stem cells of amniotic fluid—"

"Please," I say, as if being polite will persuade him. "Return my skin so I can go home." If he would cooperate, if he would listen, then we could be on the same side. I understand "we," that is how our pod thinks and solves problems, but this man wants something and it is different than what I want: to bring our stolen member back to the pod.

He rises, hands clenched by his side, pacing. His boots beat the floor. "I chose you," he says, finally. "You are beautiful. Your eyes are kind. Not like the other humans on this outpost."

Does it matter whether he chose me or whether my skin was merely the closest? My hands clench into fists, unconscious echo.

"But it's more than that." He faces me, forces his hands to unclench. My body sees that this is hard for him. "This place is my last chance." He swallows. "I'm a soldier. Everyone in this outpost is. We put in our time for a meaningless war and then we're allowed to retire here." He shook his head. "Even if I left, others will come, figure out how to recreate the pelt-sy. How to live on this planet. But we can figure it out together, if you'll help me."

My mouth moves, but it is so dry that it's hard to urge words out. "We tried to help you, we said your bodies were too fragile."

"Right." He sat down across from me, grabs one of my hands, but he did not ask permission. The touch is overwhelming, the way this body responds. We do not do that.

"Who knows how long the labs will take figuring out how to make the pelt-sy? Some of us thought that we could create it another way. That the offspring of," he rushes through, "one of you with one of us would have the best of both worlds. You know?"

The human part of me tries to parse meaning from his words, but the animal in me recognizes desperation. He reeks of a rotting fish.

The kitchen faucet bursts to life and I stand from the chair, rush to the white froth pouring out. "Saltwater." I dip my hands in, splash my face, and gulp at the stream so the familiar taste is on my tongue when I announce, "The sea comes for me."

"No. That's ridiculous." He pushes past me and turns the faucet knobs one way and then the other, but the water won't stop. "Stupid equipment. Maybe a bad pump? I'll check the well head and the casing. They gave us outdated equipment when they dropped us off on this rock."

He leaves the room, it's called kitchen, I know, and does not tie my hands. Why should he? This body, like his, is too fragile to go outside.

I go to the sink, stand there watching with a sense of satisfaction.

"You shouldn't be here." The voice has too many emotions for my limited experience in this body. The statement is, somehow, a command and an entreaty at once. Not something that someone born a human could produce.

I turn toward the speaker. They look like an older human female in a dress that hangs too large on her gaunt frame. Her skin is brown like sediment that clouds the water when the tentacled *dreer* rise from their hiding places. White hair interlaces down the back. A braid, my mind supplies. Her eyes are blue and sad. I imagine that she cries a lot. Her hands have calluses, flesh building up from repeated actions, not from swimming in the sea. Not from playing in the waves, not from dancing in the rosy light of Big Sister and Little Sister.

Something new flutters inside of me like butterfly wings tickling my ribs. I have never seen a butterfly, but this memory of a form with colorful membranes is exactly what I mean. I would like my pod to experience being such an amazing amalgam of scales and hairs and beauty. They would like the harmony. No, we would like the harmony.

Distracted by my mistake, I take a deep breath.

"I'm here," I say, and that butterfly sensation startles me again, "because of you. We didn't forget."

Their chin, her chin, who is she now, anymore?

"You waited so long," she says, "I didn't think anyone would come."

"We have missed you every moment and we sang for you." I swallow because I am happy and I am proud. "And now you can come home."

"They took away my *pelli*." She makes the right sound with the human mouth. "They sent it to a lab. I can never change form again."

Steps announce Flick's arrival with enough time for her to slip into the adjoining room so he does not see us talking.

The sound of the water running is a constant *shhhh* in the background. This is soothing to me, but he is frustrated. "I've put in a work requisition. Hydraulics aren't my specialty, but someone will be here in the morning." He kneels and opens the cabinet, using a wrench against the pipe. The saltwater shooting from the faucet slows to a drop.

"What is a lab?" The word was too foreign. He'd said it earlier and then she/they said it, but the image that fills this mind makes no sense.

"You've been talking to Lucy." It takes me a moment to realize that this set of syllables has been assigned to the woman in the other room. He stands up and puts his hands on his hips, wrench still in his hand. "Fine. Scientists. They have to figure out what the pelt-sy was made from and the only way to do that was to cut it open. Our survival on this planet means understanding alien technology and then replicating it. But it's taking too long." He scoffs. "We're not exactly a priority for the off-planet politicians."

My stomach drops and I feel dizzy, reaching out a hand to the chair. This body shocks me with picture after picture of what the lab is doing, destroying, desiccating. Our *pelli* is so integral to our being and these newcomers stole it and allowed, no demanded, other newcomers to rip our *pellis* apart.

I look through the doorway. Lucy is there. She is watching me with her hands clasped together and her chin wobbling. This is why she has given up.

"We need a new plan." He is still talking. "I need my children to have selkie blood so they'll understand the sea. No worries about being drafted in the never-ending war. This is the only way that my family survives. I need our future. That's the only thing that's kept me going through the Hell I've been through."

Little Sister winks in the middle of the window. I look over at Lucy and see her eyes widen as she begins to understand why I was captured tonight.

"Listen, I know that you don't understand, but you're so beautiful. The color of your skin, the shape of your mouth, the size of your eyes. You could save me." Dropping to his knees, wrench clattering to the floor, the soldier grabs at my dress. "Please. I love you."

This is yearning and it is not something I knew before. The force of it makes me want to give in, to agree to whatever will make him stop asking. I think of my pod and our decision to rescue the being he calls "Lucy" and that allows me to feel sad for him, but also to shake my head and pull my dress away from his grasping hands.

"Lucy learned to love her husband and she had a child. It didn't survive, but we know more now. Trust me, I'll take care of you if you do what I say."

I can't meet his eyes.

"I'll see to your room." Flicks leaves and I turn to the woman who had her skin stolen, was married to a stranger, and then forced to have a child.

"Do you want me to embrace you?" I ask.

She nods and I hug her, letting her clutch back at me.

"I'm sorry we had to wait so long."

She steps back. "You had to wait for Little Sister." Part of her still understands the push and pull of the currents.

"Yes."

"It's too late for me. This body has trapped me and I've grown old." She holds up her wrinkled hands. "But I know where he put your *pelli*."

She scrambles onto the countertop and reaches up high to pull out the sack. She drops it down to me and I pull at the cord wrapped around it.

My skin. Saltwater falls from my eyes. Soft as I remember, pliable and jelly-like. It has not dried out. I bury my face in the fur and inhale the musky, wonderful scent. This close, I hear the echo of my pod and know they are dancing beyond the black teeth, making a plea to Little Sister. Each moment Little Sister is moving away. Soon we will not have the power of the water to help us.

I think about her words. There are no other voices to talk to about this decision. No pleasure in consensus. She is more experienced on land than I am, knows more about this situation, and she tells me to go. And inside me there is an eagerness to leave, to rush back to safety and to the pod.

But I cannot leave without the podmember that he calls Lucy because she is my sister, my mother, my aunt, my daughter. That's why we agreed that one of us would be captured.

She releases a long moan when I replace my *pelli* and hand the bag back to her.

"I will not leave you," I say. "Unless we can both go."

⚘

He takes me to a room for sleeping. There is a narrow cot and a desk with a chair and a dresser against the far wall. When he closes the door, I wrap my arms around myself and sink to the floor. It is so hard and so cold and so lonely. I have never been alone like this. No sounds of the ocean lull me into dreams, there is no music, there is no comforting mental touch of the other pod members.

A sound on the door makes me look up.

Lucy is there. "May I come in?"

When I nod, she closes the door and comes closer. "May I embrace you?"

Again, I nod.

She helps me to the cot and pulls a blanket up to my chin, she makes soothing sounds that mean nothing in the newcomer's language, but could be the clicking claws of a *caer* or the cheerful screech of a *porphin*. She pulls the chair next to the cot and sits beside me as Little Sister, and our plan, drown in the deeps.

⚘

In the morning he takes me to the lab. This is the first time I've been so close to their camp. There are several small metal buildings like the one we were in last night and a larger one in the center. That is where we are headed. Clouds shift overhead and the wind sweeps my hair. The crash of the ocean is there, the water calls to me.

Inside the large white room are large machines crewed by five more newcomers. Immediately their needs and wants hammer at my mind. We teach our children not to do this, but these creatures are emotional toddlers, undisciplined with their pain and their demands. They give no thought to the group, only to themselves.

"Is that one of them?" A female with yellow hair cut short. She wears the same clothing as the other newcomers, but her frame is smaller and her voice is higher. The violence in her tone grates against me.

"Nice, Flicks," another one says. He, this human body tells me, has glasses that sit on scars racing down his cheek to disappear under the collar of his shirt. His leg is different, a curve like part of a shell, but he uses it to move around with what appears to be little hindrance. We would do something similar with our *pellis*. I think these changes must be from the war that Flicks told me about. "Is she friendly?"

"Does it matter?" says the yellow-haired one.

They choose silence, but their secrets pulse at me. Embarrassment, gratitude not to be me, implicit us versus them. I am the them.

Flicks holds up the sack with my *pelli*. "I thought we could test it against the ones we've been synthesizing."

"Great," the one with scars and glasses says. He moves to a tank, places his hands into over-sized gloves, and then plunges them into the tank. Then he holds up what looks like the body part of a tentacled *dreer*: clear and slippery and the size of a human's torso. "We've grown this so far, but if one of us tries on the real *pelli*, then we can compare." He looks to the yellow-haired girl. "Abby, you're the smallest."

"Yes." She makes a fist and pulls it close to her side in a celebratory move. "Thank you, Cap."

I double over in pain as my stomach cramps. Abby's searing sense of pride, Cap's biting curiosity, Flick's hope all swirl around me like phantom touches. Human words ricochet around my mind and I grasp at them as if I had fins instead of fingers.

Flicks takes out my *pelli*. The edges are curling up. It needs saltwater. He offers it to Abby. "Try it on."

My mental fins turn into claws to snatch up words. I've never had to do this before, to push back against these overwhelming wishes, but I do it now.

"No." I straighten against the cramping in my middle. "No. You will not give away my *pelli*. It is not yours to give. It is mine."

I feel the shock from all directions, but I don't care. I dismiss their feelings. This is unheard of in our colony, but I cannot think about it now. Worse is the violation that these newcomers propose.

"Give it back now." I step forward and hold out my hand. It shakes as my heart bangs against my ribcage so hard that the internal sound muffles my hearing.

"Oh. She's angry." Abby shrugs one shoulder as if I don't matter. "Lucy's never done that before."

"They are different creatures of the same species," Cap says, as if he has any idea. "They will have individual reactions to stimuli, but each interaction brings new information."

Flicks looks at me and shoves my *pelli* back in the bag. "We can discuss this later," he says to me. He smiles and his teeth gleam white.

A sound from one of the machines breaks the standoff and the crew returns to their devices. There is a cone-shaped alarm on top that swirls around three times and then quiets. A series of long and short sounds follow, like a *caer's* six limbs tapping against a rock at low tide.

"Ugg," Abby says when the tapping stops. "Typical check-in." She shakes her head. "No reaction to any of the reports we've sent."

Cap places his hand on her shoulder and squeezes. "As soon as they know that human life is sustainable on this planet, they'll send more settlers."

Which means that if human life is not sustainable, then they won't? I keep my face blank. These humans are so insensitive to the emotions of another that they don't notice. Maybe Lucy and I will not be able to escape. Maybe my mission is changing.

Anger stings me inside as if I'd wandered into the tentacled *dreer*. I don't know what to do with it so I feed it until Flicks says it is time to return to our building. The wind blows stronger than before and the light is red. Lucy and I both turn to the place where the seawater strikes the rocks. Our pod is there, standing in a line, buffeted by the water, making themselves seen in order to deliver a message. They stretch their forms to reach toward Little Sister. Lucy and I stare at each other as we receive their message and butterfly wings unfurl inside me. I recognize the sensation. It is my courage. If Flicks asked again, I would say that I'd named myself Butterfly-Wings.

Once we are inside, Flicks says, "Now you understand. I need someone to help me on this forsaken planet. It's a matter of survival. And it helps that you're beautiful. It is easy for me to love you."

Lucy stands by the open door. The pod's chanting has grown louder, welcoming the storm. Rain comes at an angle, blown by the wind. Seawater invades the house, kissing Lucy's feet and then retreating, creeping farther each time. Little Sister must be listening, her volcanoes erupting as she swings close.

"You love the idea of a selkie," I say. He speaks of love but sprinkles his phrases with "me." "A woman who has no past, no needs, no demands." I push him away and he falls into the water covering the floor, soaking the back of his clothes. "But I have my own story."

He stands up, furious. I see the violence in the narrowing of his eyes as he sees the water. "This stupid planet. Flooding again. How can the tide come up so high?" He kicks at the water as if were alive and then pulls a hunting knife from his hip. The kind used to peel sealskin away from meat and blubber. He holds the blade toward my throat, hand shaking with anger because he is being thwarted. "You can't—"

He doesn't seem to know how to finish. Instead, he wants me to say that I won't leave because his needs are more important than mine. Understanding chokes me. All I can do is stare back at him.

He tosses the knife to the table and exhales as if disappointed. "Shut the door, Lucy. I've got to get sandbags." Flicks stalks away.

Lucy ignores him and grabs the sack with my *pelli*. She rips it open and lowers my skin into the seawater before handing it to me.

Fingers tingling, I strip off the human dress and thrust my feet into the skin. I pull the skin, shimmying it over my hips, forcing my fingers down the sleeves. It feels so good, but then I look at the woman he called Lucy. Being in this human body has changed me, but I choose to think of "we."

I meet her eyes while I hold the knife to my *pelli* and I make the first cut.

It isn't easy but I hold with one hand and I cut with the other. When one of our *pellis* are torn, we gather around and sing to our injured friend. Sometimes one of us will offer blood to help it grow. Growing a *pelli* large enough for two bodies has never been done before. Maybe we will sing songs about it, if we can escape.

I'm taking too long.

She comes over to help me.

Saltwater is up to our knees and Little Sister moves higher in the window. Oh, she is gloriously angry tonight.

I help Lucy slip into half of my skin. It's tight, won't fit. She's been in this body so long, life changed at the whim of a stranger.

"Leave me so you'll be safe," she says.

"Nope." The word feels fierce and defiant. I love it.

I retrieve the hunting knife.

The blade stings. I release his disappointment that I won't stay. Crimson flows down my arm and onto the outer layer of skin surrounding my friend.

The layer absorbs my cells and grows until I can pull it up to cover her shoulders. Now she takes over, massaging and singing to the skin, encouraging it to grow.

I hunker down and work my own portion of skin, kneading and grabbing with my teeth to make it stretch. The soldier and crew changed me, confused and battered me with human feelings and demands. But they will not keep me here.

The soldier returns, carrying sandbags. He splashes to a halt when he sees me with the knife, sees the woman whom he knew as Lucy changing into a sleek, gray-colored creature so similar to his home world's seal. She has dreamed of this moment while lying in the human bed night after night. The images communicate through our *pellis* and I feel her wild joy. She slips out to join the pod, to be the "we."

She can return, but my portion of the *pelli* is not large enough. I am both part of my pod and still a single voice in my own head.

"Don't come closer." I am desperate enough to saw through human flesh and bone in order to return to the sea. My body knows how to show him this truth: my lips pull back in a snarl. It is un-natural to a selkie but feels right to a human. "Am I beautiful now?"

He flinches and looks out the window to avoid my question. His eyes widen as the whole island shakes. He grabs the counter.

I slice again—cutting away my sympathy for his return to a never-ending war or his future children.

Little Sister moves past the window leaving only a red light shining through.

An alarm blares from another building in the human's outpost. He turns to face me, and I see dawning realization. "The storm. Is the island going under? Are you doing this?"

From my *pelli* I hear my pod singing a triumphant chorus as seawater churns.

His shoulders slump. "Please," he says, as if being polite will persuade me. "I didn't mean to hurt you."

Third cut. This time along my ribs. I flick the knife to clean the bit of human skin, hurling away his expectation that I will learn to love him if I have no choice.

"But, you did. Your selfishness changed me." This assertion hangs in the silence between us. "I would run for your boats, now, because there will be nothing left here." I smile at him. "It's a matter of your survival."

"No." I see his dawning realization a moment before he stumbles past me and through the door, making his way to the lab with the boats and the manufactured *pellis*.

The knife falls from my human hand and the heaviness in my chest breaks apart, beaten by butterfly wings, as I lower into a watery embrace. Thick green skin—a leviathan's—slips over my shoulders as my *pelli* alters my form to match my mind. I lower into a watery embrace. My eyes, newly large, have no trouble seeing in the dark. My claws are sharp and I am not afraid. I cannot join my pod's chorus but I can swim through these ruins. I can watch for more newcomers and tell them 'no' with my long teeth.

A Quick Getaway

Randy drives the curves of the backroad like we're on the Scrambler, the ride he works at the carnival. As he crosses over the median, hand loose on the wheel, I want to tell him to slow down, but I don't want him to think I'm a nag or he might not take me with him when the carnival leaves. He's not a great catch, but maybe I'm not either so I don't say anything when he slings an arm across my shoulder and his hand dangles too close to my chest. Foster kids don't get anything for free.

We pass a field of dry corn stalks and then a weathered wooden fence appears, running parallel to the road. The posted sign reads *Don't pick the fruit.* Randy pulls the truck over to the side, tires sinking in the grass.

"What's this?" he asks, his gaze wandering over pruned trees planted in straight lines. Golden peaches hang from low branches, begging to be picked. It's late August, the tail end of peach season.

"I've never been back here," I say. It's true. I've been with this foster family for almost a year and during that time I've worked on the farm and gone to the local high school. The carnival this week is my first opportunity to escape the unbearable loneliness.

"I'm getting one," Randy announces. His hand hovers over the ignition key, but he leaves the truck running. Instead, he moves the hand from my shoulder to my thigh, right where my cut-offs end, and squeezes. "Be ready for a quick getaway."

He laughs, but I don't. I do want a quick getaway. I want to leave a rural school where I'm the weird kid who likes to draw and has a tattoo of wings on my left bicep. I want to leave a foster family who only needs a warm body to feed and water the sheep. I want to leave a farm where they name and then kill their animals. I asked if I could plant a garden instead. They thought it was a joke.

Randy climbs the fence and then wanders, caressing the fuzz of one peach and then reaching for another. When he ducks under a branch and moves deeper into the orchard, I can't see him anymore. I look at the keys in the ignition, the air conditioner pumping stale air around the truck cabin. It smells like cigarette smoke and the sickly sweet lemonade they sell at the carnival. For a moment I imagine sliding behind the wheel, but there's no point in driving away because I would be as lonely as I am now.

A sudden breeze brings the scent of ripe peaches through the window. The rustling of the nearby cornstalks could be whispers, encouraging me to get out of the truck. Overhead, the sky is the special blue that promises Autumn is coming. My mouth waters for fruit, for eternal summer, and I choose to climb the fence, too.

I'm greeted by a single wasp flying toward my face and then veering away. Like Randy, I wander deeper into the orchard. Each of the trees is perfect, the green leaves not touched with a hint of gold or red. The fourth tree in I stop. My hand curves around a fruit so soft and delicate that the skin yields to my touch. I don't grab or twist; the peach falls into my hand. Through a crack in the skin a drop of juice rolls down the back of my hand. On instinct, I lick it. An immediate tingle begins on my tongue. The juice is difficult to describe because it's sweet, but not like the carnival lemonade. I keep the droplet on my tongue, savoring, and then press my tongue to the roof of my mouth, crushing the droplet so that the liquid coats the sides of my tongue. I shudder in pleasure.

The air vibrates with the movement of hundreds of wings. I peer around the leaves, looking for the orchard's inhabitants.

Swoosh! The branches part and Randy is there, his face smeared with peach juice. "Take as much as you want," he says, laughing, gesturing like he owns this place.

We've made a mistake. I clench my fists until the nails dig into my skin because there's something foster kids learn early. Head to the bed with the broken frame and the thinnest blanket. The nice bed is already taken. You set your garbage bag of stuff in front of that one and you're gonna get jumped. Your fault for thinking you're somebody. And this place is so nice, it belongs to someone. Hell, there was even a sign.

Randy grabs a peach off the tree, yanking with a rough motion so that leaves come off too, and he shoves the fruit into his mouth. Hands free, Randy yanks his shirt over his head and tosses it to the grass. He pulls the peach from his mouth and smears the fruit all over his chest.

"Lick it off."

I shake my head. His eyes frighten me. I've seen men drunk before, but never on peaches. I don't question it though, don't try to rationalize fermented fruit. I listen to my instincts and they say to run.

"Ow." Randy's hand claps to his shoulder. "Something stung me."

He moves his hand and a wasp falls to the grass. We stare at the live insect, a shiny black color, elegant abdomen, jointed antennae broken. The fruit droplet still in my mouth tingles. Randy stoops down and I know what he's going to do.

"Don't hurt her," I say, my words thick as I speak around the fruit juice on my tongue. "Please. She's beautiful."

"She?"

"Only female wasps have stingers," I say, embarrassed at the look he gives me. "Their stingers aren't barbed so they can sting again and again."

Randy crushes the insect between his index finger and thumb. "How's that, Ms. Science?" he asks as he wipes the remains on his jeans.

Buuuzzzzzzz.

Before either Randy or I can run, the wasps arrive. They fly past us in a living black cloud and come together into the shape of a woman with a tiny waist and antenna. My heart quivers at the alien beauty. They are all female, dangerous and full of righteous anger.

55

"You trespassed." The wasps work together so that it looks like their mouth speaks. The voice is many voices. "You ate our fruit." The woman-shape quivers with rage. "And then you killed one of us."

Randy's eyes go wide, but then he laughs. "Un-be-lievable." He lurches forward, fist cocked, and punches. The wasp woman dissolves into individuals, unhurt by his clumsy swing.

The insects surround Randy. He twists, batting his hands, but can't avoid the coordinated attack. Maybe I should feel horror, but instead I watch in fascination as his skin tightens to leather, his eyes darken, and his body shrinks. The transformation is like flipping the pages of a sketch pad quickly to make art dance into life. Randy folds in on himself until he is the size of the other wasps, but he is different. His body is yellow with red stripes, like a warning. He staggers on the orchard ground trying to work the jointed legs. One black wasp hovers in the air above him.

The rest of the wasps reform the queen, the bodies working together in practiced efficiency. Their face watches and they cross their arms over their chest.

Still on the ground, Randy's wings flutter. The hovering wasp will kill him. I would have known this even if the queen's anger didn't burn the air, even if the drop of juice didn't tingle on my tongue. Maybe the hovering wasp is next of kin or maybe this is her job within the colony.

I'm going to receive a punishment next and I only have this moment to make a decision. I remember the keys in the truck, Randy's advice about a quick getaway. I remember his hand dangling near my chest and then on my thigh, the way he shoved the peaches into his mouth and then smashed the female wasp. I keep these images in my head as I fall to my knees on the ground and scoop up Randy's new body. I hold him between my finger and thumb. His surprise turns to anger. I feel it though the juice on my tongue. His abdomen pumps repeatedly against the flesh of my thumb, but nothing happens. I told him only females have stingers. I could have explained that the stinger developed from the ovipositor, the organ for egg-laying. I squeeze. There is a crunch of exoskeleton, audible over the omnipresent buzzing. I drop his dead body into the grass and look up at the queen to see if she will accept my apology.

The queen dissolves into disorder, wasps flying ellipticals and returning, a conference, and then they reform into the quiet of consensus.

The queen accuses me. "You are still a peach thief."

Yes, my tongue is still covered with the stolen juice. I walk forward on my knees into the queen, quivering with fear and hope, and I open my mouth to the wasps. For three heartbeats there is no reaction. Then they are on my face, feet on my tongue, buzzing filling my ears, and my flesh is surrounded by the insects. Tingling, same as on my tongue, spreads from the crown of my head to my toes. I am vulnerable and exposed, intimate with the wasps in a way I'd never imagined. They know me in a way that no foster family ever has.

And then it's over. They have taken back their juice and I no longer have a connection to this garden. The absence aches like a missing limb.

"We accept your penance," the queen says, in their multi-voice. "You may leave now."

I look at the impossible blue sky, the green leaves, the wild beauty. I breathe in sun-ripened peaches. Then I look at the queen and press my hands together. If they know me, then they know what I will ask.

"But can I stay?" I throw open my arms, welcoming the pain if it means I will finally belong. "Sting me."

AT THE NIGHT BAZAAR

From the far-off center of the Bazaar, the clock tower's bells chime. Golden light appears in the shape of a large door. The Night Bazaar is open.

At the Night Bazaar

This, this magical twilight hour before the Night Bazaar opens is Orphan's favorite. Perhaps her favorite should be the hour before dawn when she wheels around scooping up the lost, forgotten, and discarded items that she collects to sell from her own tent, but no. Too much envy as she watches others leave through the golden portal, returning to their home worlds. To their loved ones. But Orphan has to wait. Someone—a parent, a family member, someone who has even a clue about who she is— could come to the Bazaar. So, instead, her favorite time is now, when hope is strongest. The sun's rays refract off the many tents that spread in a makeshift city; the smells promise everything from funnel cakes to stuffed grape leaves, incense to ointments made on a faraway moon.

Snow falls. Something on the ground bunches under the white flakes, creating a small mound. Orphan unclips the grabber that hangs off her wheelchair and presses the lever to extend the plastic pincers, tightening on the mound and lifting it from the snow. Sodden tickets from a carnival game. She cradles the pile of tickets in her hands and closes her eyes, breathing in the smell of pulp released by the disintegrating paper. First, she recognizes the desire to win, then the fierce drive of competition, and finally an overall sense of good fortune from the previous owner. Orphan exhales and opens her eyes. The tickets, like everything that Orphan claims, have a faint glow. Now anyone can feel what she feels. Orphan doesn't know if this ability to marry intangible to tangible is natural, maybe there is an entire world of people like her, but she suspects it is a by-product of living in the Bazaar. That she has developed an affinity for lost things because she is lost, maybe forgotten. Regardless, she adds the tickets to her bag. Perhaps this will be a lucky night.

From the far-off center of the Bazaar, the clock tower's bells chime. Golden light appears in the shape of a large door. The Night Bazaar is open. Like the randomness of the Bazaar's internal pathways, there is no schedule of portal connections, but Orphan clenches her hands into fists and hopes.

From her position in the main aisle, she watches the portal. It looks so easy when two women in bomber jackets and goggles step through the golden light, appearing from nothing. They are followed by a group of young mages in matching uniforms and the glowing badge that identifies each as an apprentice. More travelers pass before Talla, a handsome young woman with soulful eyes and a blue headscarf, appears. The blue complements her brown skin and dark eyes. Orphan waves in greeting, a smile breaking across her face.

Talla strides forward, an unfamiliar rucksack on her back, until she stops in front of Orphan. White flakes of snow sparkle on her headscarf and shoulders, on the soft cloth of her loose pants and tunic. Talla smells like the desert, or what Orphan imagines the desert to be like with wild wind and two scorching suns, shaggy animals with humps. Orphan has seen pictures at the art tent of Talla's world and space ships and something called Victorian England, but she hasn't experienced any of the possibilities outside of her imagination. She knows the Bazaar; it is home. But, maybe, a home shouldn't be lonely.

"Salutations." Talla bows and gives Orphan that half-smile she knows so well. "I'm glad to see you, but I can't talk. I have to find someone."

"Oh, but come with me first," Orphan blurts out. "Chef's macarons are right over here, best in the Bazaar." Frantic that Talla will leave on her own errand after so many nights of waiting by the portal, Orphan grabs for her hand. "Please."

60

Concern draws Talla's brows together.

Orphan drops her hand and wheels along the packed dirt path. The crowd is easy to navigate because most aren't stopping to look yet. They want to get deeper into the labyrinth that is the Bazaar where paths change like gears in a machine and the only constant is the clock tower rising from the middle.

A sweet smell wafts on the breeze and then she is in front of the large pastry case of Chef Bisous's stall. They are short, only as tall as Orphan in her chair, but their white hat reaches toward the darkening sky. "No, no, my friend. My macarons are not unwanted. Each is handmade." They point to colorful rows of macarons. "Tonight we have gingerbread marscapone, mint chocolate chip, and raspberry with a cream filling made with a special ingredient from Callisto. Quite costly. No freebies for you, Orphan."

Talla appears through the crowd and stands at Orphan's shoulder. Giddy, Orphan's eyes shine as she performs for her audience.

"I'm offended," she says to Chef, although she isn't. This is how the Bazaar works; bartering, slide scale of valuation, remembering what is foreign or precious to various cultures. Every night is different depending on when or where the portal opens. "Surely you have cookies that aren't perfect. Not the right shape? Maybe a little burn on the bottom?"

Talla taps Orphan's shoulder. "Listen, I have to go. It's important."

"This'll be quick," Orphan promises. "Hold on."

"My macarons are not cookies." Chef sniffs. "However, I might have one for trade."

"Now you're talking." Orphan speaks louder than she intended, wants to hurry before Talla leaves. She pulls the large bag that hangs off the side of her wheelchair onto her lap. "I have tickets to a carnival game tossed to the ground when there weren't enough for a prize, a scarf with a pulled thread, and a dress bought for something called 'homecoming dance' that was too long." Orphan reaches into the bag and hesitates over her treasures until the dress seems to hum. She holds up the dress. The tulle skirt has polka dots and the torso is silky.

"I'm sorry," Talla says, but then she starts coughing.

Chef leans over the case and makes grabby hands, but Orphan holds it away. "At least three macarons. One of each flavor."

"Too much for something no one else wants."

"You want it." Orphan adjusts in her chair, manually rotating her right hip to be more comfortable.

"Too long."

"Take it to Alliz. He owes me a favor." They are some of the many for whom the Bazaar is home: Chef and Alliz the costume maker and Apothecary. "It will look beautiful on you."

"It will." Chef pouts. "Fine." They snap open a pastry bag and slide the macarons inside. Orphan accepts the bag and takes a deep sniff. The smell makes her stomach growl with hunger. She offers the dress.

Chef holds the dress to their body and gives a thrilled little scream.

Orphan turns to Talla, triumphant, but her face falls as she sees the woman straighten from coughing, hand to her stomach and mouth twisted in pain.

"What's wrong?" Orphan's heart skips. She doesn't remember who left her at the Bazaar or when she discovered her special talent for selling junk, but she remembers meeting Talla. Her easy laugh as she set up a stall to sell the colorful rugs from her home world. Her acceptance of the wheelchair Orphan needed to navigate the crowded Bazaar. Orphan's first friend.

"I'm not contagious."

Orphan frowns and repeats, "What's wrong."

"A terrible illness is affecting my country. We traced it to a bacteria in our main water source, but not until after many people and animals had been affected. So many that my home world has run out of the cure." Her hand moves from her stomach to her chest as she struggles to inhale. "Young and old suffer with fever. We need an ingredient to make more medicine before anyone else dies."

"You're one of the sick," says Orphan. Her mind tries to process.

"I've been to the Bazaar. I have the best chance of finding someone who'll sell moganite."

Shame fills Orphan and she berates herself. So anxious to show off for some stupid macarons.

"I'll lead you to Apothecary's tent," Orphan says. "What do you have to trade?"

✳

Apothecary's tent is along the opposite arm of the Bazaar, past the tower clock, on an uneven cobblestone path that makes Orphan feel nauseous as she jounces along. Or, that could be her worry for Talla making her feel sick. They pass a used bookstore stall with a beat-up leather recliner, clearly wanted, and an unenclosed space with two tables in an L-shape covered with chakra jewelry for various spinal configurations. A gramophone sits on the corner playing records, a saxophone solo floating out of its bell.

There! One more and they arrive at a serious-looking brown tent with flaps down for privacy. Talla holds the flap to the side and Orphan rolls inside. Immediately she is struck by the smell of spices, sharp and bitter with a hint of too-sweet. Across the back wall stretches a shelf that takes up the width and height of the space divided into three sections. A spidery script labels each of the colorful jars that line two sections of the shelf. The other section contains mortar and pestle, scales, and other things that Orphan doesn't recognize.

"What do we have here?" Apothecary lowers her glasses as she listens to Talla's stumbled explanation. Hurrying through the Bazaar stole her breath. Apothecary looks into Talla's rucksack and takes out a blue stone the size of Jumper bugs, hefting it in her hand. "That's a nice collection of Ici gems, but you'll have to come back. Selling you that quantity of moganite would use all of my stores. Mine is from Deneb. Earth lunar hasn't been to the Bazaar in weeks and Titan's isn't as potent."

Orphan cocks her head. Deneb is a mining colony. Crowds were still coming through the portal, but she hadn't noticed any in the boots or union garb that miners typically wore.

Talla shakes her head, frantic. "I can't wait for the next time. It's been two months since the portal came. My friends and family are dying. Our doctors need me to return with the moganite tonight, before the portal closes."

Orphan places her hand on Talla's arm, but keeps looking at Apothecary. "You have enough moganite for the doctors to make the medicine. And the Ici gems are enough to cover the cost."

"Yes," Apothecary says to Orphan. She is another inhabitant of the Bazaar so they know each other by reputation, but have never interacted. "Look, I won't be able to make medicine for anyone else if I sell it all. I'll sell you half of what I have. That's the best I can do. No one can guarantee what comes to the Bazaar and I don't know when I'll get new stock from Deneb."

Talla opens her mouth to argue, but Orphan squeezes her arm. "I understand. I want to give you a gift." She opens the bag. Her hand hovers over the paper tickets to a carnival game, the macarons, and the scarf. Then, sure, she pulls the scarf from her bag and offers it.

"It has a pulled thread," Apothecary says with suspicion, refusing to take the cloth. "I'm not trading anything, Orphan. I've heard about your tricks."

"Not a trick," Orphan insists. "This is a gift. Take it."

Apothecary reaches and her fingers close on the cloth. She examines the maroon scarf, turns it over, flicks the pulled thread, runs a finger over the stitching on the logo of a gryphon with mechanical claws from a school on the other side of the portal. She closes her eyes and lets out a brief combination of sigh and sob. She wraps the maroon scarf around her neck, hands shaking.

Talla starts to ask Orphan a question, but Orphan puts her finger to her lips to signal silence.

When Apothecary opens her eyes, tears shimmer. "I'll sell it to you. All of it."

❧

The peculiar ding-a-ling of a dented brass bell reaches Orphan through the noise of the Bazaar. It is her bell, hung outside her tent, and one of her first finds. The bell was made to be heard and so Orphan hears it, anywhere in the Bazaar. A client has arrived at her tent.

"Follow me. It's faster this way," she says as they leave, veering left when Talla would have gone right. "We don't need to backtrack through the center. The portal is a straight walk from my tent. You'll be home soon."

"Why did the apothecary change her mind?" Talla presses a hand to her chest as they hurry.

"Forgotten friendship."

Talla laughs, startled. "That's not what I would have expected. How did a scarf make her think of friendship?"

"Whoever was wearing it last may have been with friends or a special friend may have given it. I don't know the history of lost things." The paved road is both smooth and downhill; Orphan is glad for the change from the uneven bricks. "It's like I hear the echo. Then I help the item find its forever home."

"And you think everything has a forever home?" Talla is dragging behind so Orphan slows.

"Think of me as a matchmaker of sorts."

"Is the Bazaar your forever home?"

They turn the last corner and Orphan lets out a whispered curse. She both wants to and doesn't want to answer Talla, but now there's a complication.

Two cats, one a grey tabby in spectacles and top hat and the other a striking calico wearing a tuxedo jacket, stand on their hind legs outside of her tent. Each is tucking away an elaborate silk parasol that must have been used to protect someone from the snowflakes. Orphan suspects her guest's identity and wonders if she and Talla can slip away without being seen.

"At last," says Tabby, dashing Orphan's hope.

"You're here," says Calico.

They speak in unison. "We present...Lady Tybalt." The tabby uses a paw to draw back the tent's flap.

"We've heard much of your wares and decided to see for ourselves." A white cat, Himalayan Persian with the distinctive thin "M" mark on her forehead, fluffs her elaborate ball gown and strikes a pose in the tent's opening. Orphan recognizes Alliz the costume maker's artistry. "Perhaps we will buy a little gift for ourselves. No doubt this upcoming holiday season we will receive treasures and delicacies and gowns of questionable fashion, all costing more than you could comprehend. But, we are looking for something special." The ornate collar at her neck boasts nine jewels, one for each Life she still has.

"I'm...honored." Orphan struggles to switch gears from the problem on Talla's world. Everyone at the Night Bazaar knows Lady Tybalt, consort to the tyrant cat king. Theirs is a home world of court intrigue and strife that sometimes bleeds into the Bazaar. The bleeding is literal; cat's claws are sharp. "Forgive me for not standing. I don't have an extra Life to spend on healing."

If she notices the hint of sarcasm, Lady Tybalt ignores it. Instead, she smooths her whiskers with a white paw and steps deeper into the tent with a tilt of her head that suggests she will reveal more only when they are alone.

Orphan looks at Talla and lowers her voice. "Sorry I can't go with you. Keep following this smooth path and when it curves around, you'll be on the main road to the portal. It's not far."

"Thank you so much." Talla grips her sack of moganite. "You've saved my country."

Embarrassed, Orphan shrugs, but Talla doesn't stop. "You saved me."

"We're friends. That's what we do, right?" But Orphan already feels Talla's absence.

"Come through the portal with me."

This is not the first time Talla has issued the invitation. Still, Orphan laughs it off. "My wheels won't travel over your sand."

"We have flying carpets, you know. We're not uncivilized."

Lady Tybalt interrupts. "We are waiting, little queen of garbage..."

"Oh." Orphan's cheeks burn, but she answers Talla by reciting the line that has become habit. "Someone might come looking for me. Maybe next time."

Talla shakes her head. "One day there won't be a next time." She walks away without looking back.

Orphan stifles the urge to cry.

With three leaps the tabby cat has left his post by the tent and passed by Talla, only to whip around and point the parasol at her chest. "You can't leave," he says. "Go back to the tent."

Rolling forward to intercede, Orphan is stopped by the other guard cat's head shake of warning.

Talla pushes the parasol to the side with the flat of her hand and says, "What do you mean?"

"We didn't give you permission to leave," Lady Tybalt says, swaying back and forth so that her dress makes a swishing sound.

"No one leaves until Lady Tybalt leaves," Tabby says. "Her presence is a secret and will remain so. It's a matter of court security." He tucks the parasol under one arm and extends the claws of his other paw. The tips are curved and sharp. The warning is clear.

Uncertain, Talla looks to her friend. Orphan has heard of bloody catfights in the Bazaar and doesn't doubt that these guards would fight. She doesn't want Talla hurt. "I won't be long with Lady Tybalt," she says.

Talla's shoulders slump, whether in defeat or exhaustion it is difficult to tell. "I need to rest anyway."

"Excuse me," Orphan prompts the guards, needing space to wheel through the front of her own tent.

They resume their posts, facing outward, at attention. Talla heads for a dark corner of the tent and sinks down into a bean bag chair, closing her eyes. Once she's situated, Orphan gestures in a circular motion as she begins her spiel. "Welcome. I sell anything you can imagine."

Lady Tybalt surveys the piles of forgotten toys, games with missing pieces, and broken furniture with an expression of disdain. "We've heard that you have…joy."

"That's expensive." Orphan scratches at a bandage that covers the stump below her left knee. It is long healed, the scar faded, but she keeps it covered so no one will stare.

Lady Tybalt huffs and the grey tabby leans into the tent from his guard position. "Pay her."

He flicks a coin stamped with the cat king's face to Orphan. She examines it before tucking it in a pocket. "Go get a bowl of curry."

"Payment?" The cat narrows his eyes.

"It's for Lady Tybalt; she'll pay. Better get two for her. The servings are small." Knowing that Lady Tybalt is watching the exchange, she adds, "The mango chutney adds the right flavor and the ginger is merely a suggestion. Make sure you go to the striped tent, second aisle over."

Tabby ignores Orphan to speak to the king's consort. "Ma'am?"

"We are hungry," Lady Tybalt says, her tongue darting out. "We hadn't realized it."

When Tabby's gone, Orphan rummages through a woven basket of toys until she feels a tingle. She leans forward and snags the toy, wresting it from the pile to produce a View-Master, the red plastic faded to pink.

"Look through there." Orphan turns the toy. "And slide the film circles in here. Keep trying discs until you find the right one."

Lady Tybalt smirks in elegant disbelief as she stabs the dusty film circles with a claw and holds them up to the light. Her eyes narrow. She inserts a disc. Her claw clicks the lever, again and again.

Orphan watches Talla sleep. Her chest rises in inconstant rhythm as she struggles to breathe. She needs the medicine too. Orphan feels time ticking, the big arms of the clock tower moving.

Just as the tabby cat enters, balancing two steaming bowls, Lady Tybalt lifts her skirt with her free paw and twirls around the junk tent, uncaring that others might be watching. He sets the tray down and looks up to see Lady Tybalt. After a moment of shock, he drops his eyes and retreats from the tent, backing up into a girl trying to enter.

"I've brought somethin' to trade," the girl says. She is between kitten and cat, so thin that her ribs show along her sides and one of her ears is tattered as if it had been bitten. Her collar shows she has only two Lives left. Orphan guesses the kittencat is from Lady Tybalt's home world, but possibly a mixed bloodline. That's how Orphan is too. She looks humanoid, but has nothing to show which home world her parents might have been from. "We found it after the last Bazaar. Mama said it was good." She opens her paw to reveal a plastic chess piece.

"Hmm. A white knight. What do you want for it?"

"Mama said to bring back food. Or money." The kittencat swallows. "For food."

What good is having nine Lives if you still die for being poor? Orphan unclenches her jaw and calls out in a too-sweet voice to Lady Tybalt, "Do you want your dinner?"

Lady Tybalt drops the View-Master and takes a step toward the bowls. She sniffs the air and then ignores the food; instead, she presses the toy back to her eyes.

"I said, do you want your curry?" Orphan already knows the answer. Her hands are on the bowl and she is able to claim it.

Lady Tybalt yowls in pleasure. She is lost to everything but herself.

Pocketing the white knight, Orphan extends the bowl to the kittencat. "Take this."

Eyes wide, the kittencat shakes her head. "I can't. That's too much."

"Well, it would be too much if you'd found a pawn, but this guy is my favorite. He can move in unexpected ways." Orphan reaches into her bag and pulls out the pastries from Chef. "So, I guess I owe you these, too." She winks.

Whiskers trembling, the kittencat accepts the bowl and pastry bag and hurries away.

The tuxedoed calico peers in. "That was Lady Tybalt's food!"

Orphan stares down the cat. "When it became junk, it became mine."

Calico pulls back her lip to expose a long tooth. "You knew that would happen. You tricked her into paying and then made her forget about it."

Orphan pushes against her seat so she can readjust. "It's not my fault if she no longer wants it."

The fur on her body stands on end so the cat looks larger, but Calico withdraws to her post.

Orphan exhales and then takes a deep breath in. The remaining bowl of food smells delicious, spicy and a little sour, and her stomach rumbles with hunger. Ignoring the sensation, Orphan wakes Talla. "Eat."

She moans in appreciation. "From the striped tent?"

"Of course. I only serve my guests the best."

Talla stops with the spoon halfway to her mouth. "Where's yours?"

"I've already eaten," she lies.

Talla only finishes half of the bowl before she sets it aside. Her brown skin has sweat across the hairline. Orphan feels her forehead. The skin is so much warmer than it should be. Is that crackling sound from her lungs?

"Not much longer," Orphan promises. "The disc is almost done."

Lady Tybalt brings the View-Master down, panting. Foam from her wild exertion dots the corner of her mouth. "I want another disc."

"No." Orphan shakes her head. "Joy without work is addictive. It's strong as a drug. I've seen it before. It's too easy and then—"

"I need another disc." Lady Tybalt ends with a wild yowl.

The tent curtain twitches open as the tabby cat peers in.

"Pay her," Lady Tybalt hisses. "Give her the whole bag."

The cat sweeps his top hat off. "Lady—"

"Do it," she snarls, the foam dripping.

The moneybag rattles against the rickety tray with the half-empty curry bowl.

Lady Tybalt examines each disc, tossing each away until one catches her attention. She covers her face with the View-Master and dances again.

Talla groans, her dark, soulful eyes open. "Promise me you'll take the moganite to my world."

Orphan's heart cracks open. "I won't. You're going to be fine. You'll take the first dose."

"I knew I had the infection bad, but I thought I had more time." Talla pulls her headpiece to the side so that dark hair spills out. Her eyes roll back in her head; her body slumps to the side like a puppet with cut strings. "I had to see you again."

"It's finished." Lady Tybalt looses a howl of rage. "I've seen everything on this one too."

"Get out," Orphan says, voice thick with unshed tears. "Talla needs joy more than you."

"I want to dance." Lady Tybalt's white fur is grimy with sweat, dust, and the dirt created by her swirling. "I have the king's ear. You must do what I say or he'll bring the whole army to rip you apart."

Orphan wants to scream with the agony of her friend dying, wants to understand why someone else from Talla's world hadn't come to get the moganite, why Talla hadn't told her she had to get to the portal immediately.

I had to see you again. Could it really be that simple?

Orphan looks around her tent at all the treasures she's collected while waiting at the Night Bazaar. The familiar glowing string of lights from some world's holiday that wrap the top of her tent. The calligraphy set with a pen that leaks. The robot hedgehog. These things have been her version of a family.

"You want another disc?" Orphan says. Negotiation is her specialty, but she is lightheaded at her own audacity. "It'll cost one of your Lives."

"Never!" The attendants rush inside. "The king would never—"

"He'll scratch your eyes out," says Tabby.

"He'll burn your tent to the ground," says Calico.

"He'll string his violin with your guts," they say together.

"Stop," Lady Tybalt demands. "Leave us."

The attendants drop to all four paws and dash away, surely to return with the king's soldiers.

"A human cannot use a cat's Life." Lady Tybalt's pink tongue darts out. "It's worthless to you."

"It's my gift. I can take your junk and make it a treasure." Orphan has never tried this before, doesn't know if the Bazaar will allow it, but she will make it be true through force of will. She has never wanted anything as badly as she wants this.

Lady Tybalt shrugs as if a Life means nothing.

Ping.

A jewel drops from her collar.

Orphan picks up the jewel and presses it to Talla's left temple.

Lady Tybalt drops to all fours and springs onto Talla's chest. Her ears flatten and she breathes into Talla's face. Her whiskers twitch and she breathes into Talla's face again. This time a smoky bubble forms from her mouth and then retreats down Lady Tybalt's throat. She kneads Talla's chest with her claws as if finding purchase and breathes a third time. A smoky form emerges from her mouth and hovers in the air over Talla.

Lady Tybalt leaps away, bored.

Orphan reaches out a trembling hand to guide the Life closer. Her body tingles with something like electricity, but that leaves a smoky taste on her tongue. She imagines walking through the air, no, spinning through the air like liquid lightning melting upwards. Heat spreads through her limbs and she cannot hold this Life any longer. It wants to expand inside of her, fill her, but Orphan is not empty.

View-Master discs fly as Lady Tybalt scavenges. She inserts a new disc and dances, her movements wild and uncoordinated.

Orphan shakes Talla. Talla inhales, chokes, and sits upright. Sparks flicker over Talla's body; her hair floats out from her head.

"What?" Talla's fingers scrape and pull against her skin. "What's happening?"

The sounds of a commotion come from the main aisle of the Bazaar. It is easy to imagine martial cats racing through the portal

71

toward her tent. *Scratch your eyes out. Burn your tent. String his violin with your guts.*

"Almost daybreak. You need to get to the portal before it closes."

Talla rewraps her headscarf. "Ready."

Orphan wheels out the front of her tent and reaches deep into her bag, hand tightening on the carnival tickets when they tingle, full of potential to win.

The tower clock sounds, a wave of vibration spreading through the Night Bazaar.

Orphan holds the tickets up into the air, feeling the wind try to pluck them from her grip.

Cats in leather armor turn the corner, led by a Captain in a helmet racing straight toward her tent.

Orphan releases. The tickets scatter like dandelion seeds.

A nearby person snatches one up. Immediately a growing crowd scrambles for the tickets, desperate for a chance to win. The cat soldiers slow down, bogged by the bodies between them and the junk tent.

"She's right here," Talla calls, bringing Lady Tybalt out of the tent and into the false dawn. The cat's fur is matted and dirty, the View-Master still clutched in her paw. "It would embarrass the king if anyone saw her like this, right?"

The Captain slides to a halt, his gaze going from Lady Tybalt to Orphan. Talla releases Lady Tybalt and the cat wanders back into the tent, out of sight.

The Captain snaps at the air in anger. "We'll be waiting for you. Every time that portal opens. We'll wait." Then he follows Lady Tybalt, motioning to his soldiers to join him.

"Race you to the portal," Orphan calls to Talla as she wheels down a side aisle and then cuts over to the main path. Orphan waves at Chef, doesn't answer their confused, "Where are you going?"

Others are hurrying too; they don't want to be trapped on this side.

At the last moment, Orphan rubs her palms against her wheels like brakes. She stares at the golden light. Her heart beats so fast. She loves the Night Bazaar. She loves the mystery, the smells of foreign food, the way every night is different. This is home.

Talla rushes up clutching the life-saving moganite, her dark eyes holding Orphan's. She is only one foot from the portal. "I have to go," she says.

"You promised to show me the Library of Sinking Sands."

Talla gapes and Orphan almost laughs. She feels it inside, a frightened effervescence threatening to spill out.

"What changed?"

Orphan's cheeks burn, but she manages, "Someone came for me."

Words gush from Talla. "We can look for your parents, for your family, if you want. It'll be my turn to help you. Or, I can take you to the Library first, or we have this amazing—"

"Plenty of time to decide once we're through."

Talla nods. She takes a step back and disappears into the golden light. There's a flicker of blue sky and then nothing but the empty portal.

Orphan closes her eyes and pictures that flicker of blue sky. She imagines traveling through the portal to all the worlds she's seen in the books in the tent by the tower clock. She imagines not being alone. No more waiting. She wheels into the welcoming light, her whole body tingling like she is found.

Saving Money

*Y*ou watched this "reality" show about extreme couponing where the people collect piles of newspapers and sort and research and then buy sixteen boxes of spaghetti noodles to save $5. They are doing it all wrong. First of all, anyone who eats sixteen boxes of spaghetti before the expiration date is going to have the kind of problems that $5 won't fix.

More important, though, the way to save money is not to stock up but to pare down. This struck you the first time someone said you look like you live in your car. Back then you were commuting over an hour to college. Then you went straight to your lame job. Anything you needed for the day had to be packed. So, yeah. You kept snacks and drinks in your car for between classes, took your laptop everywhere, had sweatshirt, extra shoes, and a couple changes of clothes.

Why, you thought, should I pay rent on a third of an apartment? Yours was the smallest room anyway. Not much bigger than a car. BAM! Now you live in a mobile unit. Can drive close to the college and park under the welcoming parking lot lights of a Walmart. Miss all the morning traffic. Wake up, use the store bathroom to change clothes, brush your teeth, and you are on your way.

Eating fast food adds up quickly. A downside of not having a kitchen in your car. But why do you need a kitchen when so many restaurants have kitchens? Have too much food? Why should you spend time grocery shopping, dicing, preparing, measuring, eating, cleaning up, when there is an obvious solution. Some people call it dumpster diving. At first even you were unsure. Would you have to climb inside a smelly dumpster? Would you get stuck inside? Would you find a dead body like in all those crime shows? But, now that you live in your car, you can drive around and spy on your local favorite restaurants. Follow a pattern. That's using your college education.

Take Luigi's Pizza, for instance. A pizza bar, they call themselves. All kinds of pizza pies set in a row like a salad bar and customers can take a slice of this or a slice of that. Clean up is a kid in a cheap uniform dumping uneaten slices into a garbage bag. Their back door opens into an alley. Nothing to stop anyone from walking down the alley, maybe hanging out against the wall. About 40 minutes past closing time, the door opens and the bag gets tossed. A bag that ends up in your car. You've had pretty good luck finding the bag full of pizza, but not always. Opening the other bags of trash, even if you don't have to dig in them, requires finding a bathroom to wash your hands. Purell won't do for that kind of stench.

Food and shelter costs are down, but the human spirit becomes bored. The soul longs for luxury and comfort. This is the third leg of your master savings plan. Head to model homes for a day of relaxation without the clean up. You find it easy to spot these neighborhoods. Built in radiating circles away from the city, a model stands alone, maybe a couple wooden frames going up on the other side of the street. The freshly mowed corn fields look like a military haircut. The subdivisions all have names like "Meadow Bright" and "Lark's Landing" and "Whispering Glen." You walk in there, take a water from the fridge, a cookie from the plate. Sometimes, the most desperate places will have cheese and crackers with little red moons of pepperoni around the outside of the platter.

"Please sign in," the realtor will say. You will. With a fake e-mail address. The toilets upstairs are all wrapped up like Christmas presents. If you want to use one, you must go down to the basement. That's alright. After a tour, you always settle in the basement anyway. In these houses the basements are like a whole different house. They are the recreation rooms of the imagination. Helped by the fake glasses of wine placed strategically about. You like to turn these up-side down. Watch for reaction.

When the real estate agent comes looking for you—leaning back in the easy chair or settled into the movie theater room showing a new release—he or she will have a tentative smile.

No, you'll say, you don't need anything.

Maybe the agent, if crass, will ask if you have enough money to be here.

Of course, you say, I've been saving.

1416 DEFORESTED LANE

Jarilo pulls the reins and the horse lowers his head, bit between the teeth, and paws the ground.

1416 DeForested Lane

Roger, dressed in white slacks and a cashmere sweater, gives the father a tight smile as he welcomes the man to the open house. *It only takes one customer to make the sale and then I can go home.* Roger wants to return to Ted, his lover. So, Roger is willing to suspend judgment when he sees the family of potential buyers.

"Welcome," says Roger. "I'm Roger." He pronounces it the American way, with an "r" sound instead of an "h."

"Perun," the father says. He is a hoary, hairy man with what looks like two days growth of grayish-white on his face, creeping down his neck. Black hairs spring from the neck of his stained t-shirt and a silver necklace with a lightning bolt nestles in the hair. Blue jeans are baggy and Roger hopes they won't fall down. As if in answer, the man hitches them up by the belt loops. He will do this many times throughout the tour of the house.

Roger guesses this word, "Perun," is the man's name, but has no clue whether it is first, last, or middle. His skin, the part not covered by hair, is white and crevassed rather than lined. He gives the impression of being a man of the people. If the people are work-worn, slightly downtrodden, possess dirty fingernails, and are still strong as a Slavic ox.

79

"My two daughters." Perun speaks with a heavy accent and obvious pride.

Roger shoots a discreet glance to the golden ring on Perun's fourth finger. One article in "Real Estate Unlocked" advised remembering the phrase *Happy Wife, Happy Life,* but Roger is, of course, aware of the irony in assuming a hetero partner. "Will your wife be joining us?"

"Which one?" Perun laughs so Roger laughs too. The article has not prepared him for that answer.

"Anyway, nice to meet you." Roger steps to the side and uses his left arm to usher the family inside. "Welcome to my house."

1416 DeForested Lane is an exquisite beast. Bigger and grander than houses near the city, it sprawls alone in what used to be a cornfield. Until now, no one comes to view it. The site is too far away from the city, accessible only by gravel road, and the rest of the community won't be built until money has changed hands.

Although the man said "two" daughters, Roger is confused because he sees three females, two standing and a baby carriage with a pink blanket hanging over the edge.

"Hello," Roger says to the teenaged ice maiden who could model furs on the covers of fashion magazines. She'd have to be photographed in black-and-white to give her starkness its due: white-blond hair, the light blue eyes, black eyebrows, bright red lips. And, she'd have to stop crying. The continuous tears would be bothersome to potential fur buyers. She doesn't seem to be bothered though, raising a handkerchief every so often to blot the trails.

The other girl is much younger, maybe 4th grade, like Ted's niece. Her hair is in two braids and she smiles at Roger, revealing that one of her front teeth is still growing in.

"Watch this," she says. With a sudden movement, she throws her hands at the floor and her feet go overhead, and before Roger knows what she's about, the girl is cartwheeling down the hallway, head over heels over head.

Roger gasps.

"Is okay," Perun says, but it's not a question. It's a statement obfuscated by his heavy accent that causes him to skip over the 't' sound.'

Still, Roger understands. He doesn't want to offend Perun. "Of course. I wasn't worried about the artwork on the walls or the vase in the corner with the flowers. My only concern was for your little girl." Roger searches Perun's face for signs of wealth, for signals of interest in buying the model, for any scrap of hope that this meeting will lead to Roger's escaping the model house. "Shall I show you the kitchen? Granite countertops and the newest Energy Star appliances."

Perun grunts, a sound from deep in his belly that causes the wiry black hair at the top of his shirt to vibrate.

The ice maiden pushes the baby carriage. It isn't like the strollers that Roger is used to seeing in the city, the slick plastic models with tires that zoom over curbs or on running paths. This is an early model perambulator such as one would see in the early 1900's being wheeled about in Kensington Park. The child must be sleeping because the top is down. The wheels click on the hard wood floor as Roger leads the way to the kitchen. He keeps a smile in place. *The cleaning service will scrub the marks away tonight.*

"Please fill out the information card on the kitchen island with your contact information. And, I'll give you my business card when you leave in case you think of any questions."

Roger has been reading about ways to convince buyers to close the deal on residential properties. He has a lot of time alone sitting in the office of the model home, surrounded by samples of carpet, brick color for the outside, and wooden floor planks with both beveled and straight edges. Every morning, after the 95 minute drive from the city, Roger bakes chocolate chip cookies in the oven and then opens the oven door and turns on the fan to pump the smell through the kitchen. Fresh flowers go in the vase on the kitchen table.

Turning off the fan so he won't have to raise his voice, Roger extends the plate of cookies to Perun.

Whack! The top of the baby carriage snaps back. A bonneted head stares out.

"Where are your manners, young man?" The voice is an angry screech. "Who doesn't offer food to oldest first?"

Roger feels that his mouth is open, he knows he must close it, but he cannot look away from the tiny old woman wearing an old-fashioned dressing gown. *She must be over 100 years old.* Inside the bonnet, her face appears to float, large and moonish, in the sea of blankets.

"Babushka," the ice maiden says to the old woman, but it seems an acknowledgement rather than a reprimand. To Roger she says, "Grandmother is grumpy when she wakes up. Low blood sugar."

"I'm so sorry," Roger stutters. He is at a loss, his prepared tour speech forgotten. The ice maiden, still crying, takes the plate and offers it to the old woman. Babushka grabs a fistful and stuffs them into her mouth, crumbs dropping onto the blanket. Unappeased, she glares at Roger.

He says, "Perhaps you'd care for a beverage? We have bottled water and juice boxes."

Babushka crinkles her fingers at him in the universal "gimme" gesture. Feeling Perun's eyes on him, Roger brings forth a juice box and holds it out to the baby carriage. The old woman grabs at it, stabs in the plastic straw, and sucks down the fruit medley. With a burp, the old woman throws the juice box out the side of the carriage and settles back. The ice maiden closes the top of the carriage.

"We will see the house now," Perun announces.

There is a thump from the conservatory and Roger, wild-eyed, looks for the cartwheeling daughter. "I'm alright," she calls from that direction.

"This way," Roger says. He feels light-headed. The ice maiden parks the carriage in the kitchen. Faint snoring can be heard. Roger assumes the old woman will call out if she awakens. She seems to have a healthy set of lungs.

As the family examines the master bathroom—the cartwheeling girl has joined them, but Roger doesn't know how she got up the stairs—Roger's phone vibrates. Ted. Roger fights the urge to answer. He doesn't want to jeopardize the sale.

Perun pulls at the wire shelves of the walk-in closet. To Roger's left is a two-person shower. Both the ice maiden and the cartwheeler are in there. He hopes they don't turn it on. Across the bathroom, the sunken tub is next to a bay window overlooking the mowed cornfield. Beyond the field, the dark line of trees marks the boundary of the property owned by the company.

Pushing past Roger, Perun steps to the bay window. With a "snick" sound, the window's lock releases. Sticking his head out, Perun yodels, calling out foreign words in a sing-song voice. The ice maiden wanders from the shower and presses up against another pane of glass. Father and daughter stare out over the mowed field toward the dark line of trees.

"Who are you calling for?" Roger jokes.

The cartwheeler stops playing with the foaming soap at the sink. Cranberry-Melon-Persimmon scent makes Roger's nose twitch. "He's calling for Jarilo so Morana will stop crying."

"Oh," says Roger. "Is that your dog? Did he run away?" He is creating a story from sparse facts to explain this strange family.

The girl laughs so hard that she covers her mouth and bends over holding her stomach.

Roger thinks this is melodramatic and uncalled for. He knows enough, now, to step back when he sees her arms go above her head. And then she is cartwheeling out to the master bedroom and beyond to the hallway.

"All the bedrooms have their own bathrooms," he calls loud enough for Perun to hear, if the man will stop screaming out the window. To the girl in the hallway, "Watch out for the other set of stairs."

Roger is anxious to get away so he can call Ted. "Take your time looking around," Roger says to Perun's back. With the window open, a dank smell has come inside, overpowering the fake fruit of the hand soap. Fermenting leaves, though it is early spring, and a yeasty smell like homebrewed beer. The horizon is hazy as if smog from the city is creeping closer, obscuring anything beyond the trees. "I'll be downstairs if you have any questions."

On his way to the office, Roger passes through the kitchen and freezes. The carriage is where it was left, Babushka presumably asleep, but above the kitchen island circles a cloud of orange and red butterflies. Where one specimen might be considered beautiful, the current number of insects is overwhelming. Invasive. They swirl around the pendulum light like a bloody cyclone.

The closest windows are in the breakfast room and Roger rushes to close the one cracked open. *They must have come in because of the kitchen light.*

The largest butterfly peels away from the group and flies to Roger's chest. Its antenna vibrates and the wings flap in slow motion, the black insect legs hooking themselves into the minute holes of his cashmere sweater. Gripping the material, the insect crawls toward Roger's face. This close Roger can see the fur covering its black body, the shingles of its wings. Sickened, Roger flicks at the creature, but it is stubborn and won't let go. The insect creeps closer to his face.

"You have a little something on your shirt." The crying girl, Morana, stands at the railing above and looks down into the kitchen.

"I'll call an exterminator immediately," Roger says. Frantic, he cups the butterfly and yanks it off his chest, tossing the insect away as if to prevent her from seeing what has already been seen. "When the community goes up you won't have so much trouble with wildlife."

"Babushka says butterflies are witches' souls."

Roger grabs a glossy brochure of 1416 and uses it to wave through the cloud of butterflies, but they regroup after each disturbance.

"They'll die soon enough." Morana speaks as if her words have no consequence. Or, perhaps, as if her statement is the only thing of consequence.

Goosebumps raise on Roger's arms. He tries to smile and nod, and then he retreats to the office.

Behind him the ice maiden calls. "Everyone dies soon enough."

Inside the office, Roger shuts the door and hits "redial." His hands are shaking.

Ted has a small part in an off-Broadway production of "Stills of a Computer's Feelings" and Roger feels Ted has been talking about the first violinist too much. Last night Roger asked, "Why do you need a full orchestra for a play about a computer? Wouldn't a synthesizer be more appropriate?" But Ted rolled his eyes and muttered about Philistines. Which seemed ill-informed to Roger because he watches the History Channel to relax and it is commonly accepted that the Philistines had been quite cultured. But, Roger didn't want to fight. He wants to be in love.

Ted's voice sounds annoyed. "I told you I'd call this afternoon. Why didn't you answer?"

"I'm sorry." Roger hears creaking as the family walks around upstairs, but any words are indistinct.

"Why are you whispering?"

"There's a family here. They might buy the house."

84

"You shouldn't have called me back if you're so busy." Now Ted sounds angry. Roger reminds himself that anger comes from feeling hurt.

"I'm never too busy for you."

"Then you'll come to my performance tonight? Oh, Roger, I'm so glad." Ted pronounces his name the Portuguese way, and this sound from home makes Roger happy. He looks at his watch.

"I might be a little late—"

"I knew it. You don't really want to come." Ted hangs up.

Roger slides the phone away. *If I can sell this house, I'll be able to go to every one of Ted's performances. My commission will be enough for me to buy a bigger apartment. We'll be happy.*

He paces, practicing the sales pitch that he will use to get Perun to sign papers this afternoon. Opens a copy of the glossy brochure to what he considers the most flattering picture of 1416 DeForested Lance and angles it to best view from the guest chair. In the space between the end of the sales pitch and starting over, Roger realizes the absence of sound. No more footsteps. No more voices calling. He yanks up the office blinds and looks out at the one road. No car parked beside his, but the yellow excavator is still here, off to the right, slumbering in rusty stasis. A pygmy owl perches on top of the abandoned machinery. As if feeling Roger's gaze, the bird wings away.

Roger marches out and through the main house. The carriage is gone from the kitchen. Even the butterflies have disappeared. "No, no, no," he says. The family left without saying goodbye. No chance for the sit down in the office where Roger could offer upgrades and a free conservatory if Perun would sign today. No chance to bring home a commission for Ted. No chance to get away from this lonely model house in the middle of nowhere.

"Hello," Roger calls. Emptiness echoes back from the model's hallways, bedrooms, bathrooms. "Hello," he calls again. Hurrying upstairs, Roger approaches the master bathroom window. Outside the red sun sinks across the sky, a pink suggestion through the smog.

In the cornfield are what look like upright sticks in the ground. Baby trees advancing like an army from the forest toward the mod-el. *The builder must have planted them to disrupt the military haircut of the mown cornfield. I never look out at this view because the office window frames the gravel road, focus on incoming traffic. Or lack thereof.* The window doesn't want to close. The smell is stronger, dank and musky and enticing. It reminds Roger of sex, which reminds him of Ted. And the mysterious violin player. He holds his breath while struggling with the frame. With a final snick, the window slides into place and Roger locks the mechanism harder than is necessary.

Roger looks at his watch. Commission is blown. But. If he leaves now and speeds till he gets to the highway, he might tear out the undercarriage of his leased BMW, but he also might get there in time for tonight's curtain. Which would save his relationship with Ted.

He flies out the front door, locking it behind him, and tires spin on gravel. A few miles from the highway, fog hovers in the air. Roger slows the BMW, but he will not stop, cannot stop. He must get to Ted, he must get to the play. This, he feels, is his last chance to escape the model home. Which doesn't make sense because he can drive away anytime he pleases, but the family and the smell, he misses the smell already, and the marching baby trees have all affected Roger's perception. He needs to get to the city and have a drink. If he could just tell this to Ted, make it into an amusing story, the events would lose their hold on him.

His phone rings. Roger curses. He doesn't usually, but this has been a trying day. He pulls to the side of the road. There are no other cars, but he puts on his flashers because of the fog.

A hysterical woman gives him an earful of Spanish. Roger cannot keep up. He speaks Portuguese and English, but only a smattering of Spanish. Mostly the words that are the same with a different pronunciation.

Soon enough, though, Roger understands that the cleaning lady and her crew (her cousin's son) have left the model house. They went to the basement and there were people playing cards at the table down there who would not leave.

"A hoary, hairy man, an old baby, a girl doing—"

"Cartwheels," says Roger. "They were in the basement. I thought they left."

"They didn't leave. Said it's their house." The woman is angry. "We left. Union says we clean empty houses. Take it up with my lawyer."

86

As if to offer proof, a beat up Nissan drives by heading towards the highway. The woman has a cell phone pressed to her ear and her crew (her cousin's son) is in the driver's seat.

"Their house?" says Roger. "Does Perun want to buy it?"

Dial tone.

Dread settles in Roger's soul as he watches the Nissan's lights disappear. *Abandoned.*

He looks at his watch. Then he dials Ted. It's easy. He goes to the button that says "favorites" and taps the screen where Ted's face grins off-center in a circle.

"Hello."

"Ted, I'm so sorry. I'm going to be late, but I'll get there halfway through. Thought we could go out for a drink after. I have a funny story to tell you and maybe some good news—"

"Who is this? Roger?" Ted says it the American way and Roger's heart breaks. "As if I actually thought you'd come. It's too late. Cooper and I already have plans."

"Cooper," repeats Roger. "Like mini-Cooper?"

"Ad Hominem attacks via names? Declasse, Rog, de-class-ee." Ted hangs up.

Roger feels like Ted hung up weeks ago. The violinst—Cooper— is probably giggling with Ted right now, talking about him. Roger could speed toward them, but what's the point? Second best is to sell the model and tell the company he'll never work outside the city's limits again. Or, maybe he'll go home to Brazil.

He swallows his heart and turns the car around.

1416 DeForested Lane emerges from the fog and Roger is struck by how it looks like Gothic horror instead of luxurious new home. There are no still other cars, which is one reason Roger didn't realize the family was still here. Also, he called out before he left. Perhaps they didn't hear all the way down in the basement.

Angry at Ted, at the model house, at the question of where he was going to sleep—déclassé to call Ted and ask if he and mini could sleep at mini's?—Roger rockets through the house and down the basement stairs.

As the cleaning woman attested, the family is sitting in wooden swivel chairs pulled up to the card table. One chair has been removed so that Babushka can play from the comfort of her carriage. Two chairs are empty. The cartwheeling girl is going at it, singing out each revolution as she careens from wall to wall. Perun, the crying ice maiden, and grandma have stacks of poker chips in front of them.

Plastic water bottles from the upstairs fridge have been used and crushed and thrown around the room like hipster beer cans.

"The young man came back," the old woman cackles. "Libation?"

Roger addresses himself to Perun. "Is today the day to make your home buying dreams come true? I can show you the various blueprints for houses available in this community or we can negotiate to buy this model."

Perun gives a one-sided shoulder shrug. "We are here. Why should we pay?"

Babushka squeezes the juice box so that liquid arcs though the air onto the carpet.

"Stop that," Roger says. He's angry. "Are you going to buy this house or not? You've certainly made yourselves comfortable."

"Is nice house, but we already live here," Perun says. He draws a card, throws two chips into the pile, leans toward the crying girl. "Go fish."

"You can't stay here if you aren't buying it." This is not how Roger's sale pitch is supposed to go. "It's a model. I'm the representative for the company and I say you need to leave. Now." Roger swallows. Perun is big. He was older, but his arms still looked like he interned at a blacksmith's.

"What company?" says Perun. "We lived here first, in the forest. Then the machines come and disturb our home. You cut down the trees and made a mess, but you make a nice house for us."

Roger's mind spins, but he can't make sense of what Perun is saying.

The crying girl, Roger struggles to remember her name, Morana?, says, "Besides, we have to wait for Jarilo."

"Jarilo," says Roger. "Who is Jarilo? Is Jarilo going to buy this house? Who is going to buy this house." Roger hears his voice climbing in timbre, evidence of his distress. He's lost both Ted and the sales commission in one day and, in his heart, he knows that he never had either one.

88

"The boy is upset," says Babushka to Perun. "Do you think he'll cry?" She seems less concerned than curious. "I'd like your tears for libation, young man." She squeezes the juice box several times in a row. "I'm out."

Roger swallows. He feels helpless in the face of their aplomb and turns to the young girl. "If you could just stop cartwheeling."

"Why," asks the girl. She puts a braid in her mouth and chews on the hair.

"It's distracting. I can't think. Try being right side up for a while. You might like it."

"Which way is right side up?" She blinks in a double wink like a lemur or other non-innocent animal might do. Twists her neck like a contortionist. "Maybe you don't know."

Morana says, "Red club."

"Go fish," says the grandma. She pushes a stack of buttons into the middle. "I've got the Old Maid, too."

"No kidding," says Perun.

"I'll call the police," says Roger. "If you don't leave right now."

Morana gives Roger a sad smile, or maybe it only looks sad because she's crying. "Do you think they'll find us, silly boy? The house is gone. There's nothing there anymore. Come," she pats an empty chair, "come play with us until Jarilo gets here."

"Why won't they find us?" Roger says, but the answer is clawing its way up his throat, scratching the back of his eyeballs, pulling the corners of his brain down like a parachute. He runs to the French doors leading out of the basement. Blanket of white, cocoon maybe. "I've made a mistake," he says, but there is no answer.

The fog surrounds, encroaches, centered on the model house. Desperate to get away, Roger pushes through the basement "walk out" doors. The air lays heavy against his skin. The saplings appear as shadows at regular intervals suggesting ghosts rather than new life. The smell of beer oozes from the ground as if the soil's fecundity were uncontainable. Looking down, Roger sees earthworms teeming in complicated, ecstatic knots. An owl—Roger thinks the same one earlier perched on the excavator—glides overhead, wings spread out as if to touch the opposite walls of fog. In typical fashion, the owl asks "whoo" before becoming a shadow in the forest.

Roger feels a hysterical laugh bubble up. Because the answer is obvious.

From the space where the owl entered emerges a figure on horseback. Roger clasps his hands together to hide their shaking. They've been waiting for Jarilo. Who else would be riding toward the abandoned house? *But, it wasn't abandoned,* Roger corrected himself. *I'm still here.* His heart beats at the base of his throat. He steps forward, the soil sucking at his shoes with a squelching sound.

The figure—Jarilo—looms at the approach until Roger can see the horse, a blood bay with a crooked blaze down the nose. Jarilo pulls the reins and the horse lowers his head, bit between the teeth, and paws the ground. The released smell makes Roger dizzy and he holds out a hand to grasp the heavy air, asking it to support his weight. Ears laying flat, the horse whinnies. Roger has no experience with horses, but it is not too much to imagine the horse rearing, these impatient front hooves pushing him to the ground where his body would be absorbed by the mud and the ecstatic worms.

"You are Jarilo," Roger says, hating himself for the inadequacy of words. "Your family is here."

Jarilo throws a leg over the horse's withers and slides off with easy grace. This close, Roger can study the figure. High cheekbones, Slavic eyes so dark they are inner space and Roger could drown in them, floundering past stars and worlds and ancient civilizations. Jarilo wears a red cloak and riding breeches. Ginger hair brushes shoulders. In the capricious light of twilight, Jarilo's sex is indeterminate. Roger first thinks female and then male and then back to female. It occurs to Roger that Jarilo is both and neither and something else besides.

What is certain, however, is that Jarilo is the source of the fecundity seeping from the ground into the air. The pheromones are driving Roger crazy. He stands on his tiptoes to contain the intense emotions that will not be held back by the thin barrier of his skin.

"You should all go now," Roger whispers. He is confused because there is no other place to be and he wonders what he means. All that is here is now. The trees and the fog and Jarilo and the card game.

Jarilo reaches forward to clasp Roger's shoulders with fingers strong enough to leave bruises. So is her mouth as she presses it to

Roger's. There is the snick of teeth hitting and then Roger's mouth opens and he feels Jarilo's arousal through the breeches. Roger's body, or maybe his mind, is melting and floating at the same time.

The horse's whinny breaks off the intentionality of the kiss and Jarilo presses Roger's face to his hard chest. Roger is overwhelmed with sensation; he understands the butterflies in the bloody cyclone. He must circle Jarilo, panting and gasping, never stopping. Jarilo nuzzles Roger's ear. The earth smell is everywhere, buzzing inside his brain, and Roger is going to be sick, but he is distracted by the not unpleasurable sensation of a sandpaper tongue lathing behind his ears, cleaning him with mother cat's meticulous precision. Cleaning his skin and making Roger concomitantly more and less sensitized. When she stops, Roger feels a strange sense of regret.

"Shall we play?" Jarilo asks. "It's getting early."

Perun and Morana have come to the basement door, Babushka's carriage in between. The cartwheeling girl is in a handstand, her socked feet making marks on the glass. Morana has stopped crying.

"I think I've made a mistake." Roger's mouth is used to forming these words, as if the syllables are a pattern to be repeated.

Jarilo opens the door to the basement and sweeps her left hand in an ushering gesture. "Welcome to our house."

The Great Blockage

*H*elen later recalled it was her neighbor Tim who had the idea. Trash collection was only once a week and that wasn't enough. The community's cans overflowed. Wind swept through the street and the cans fell over like toy soldiers, plastic bags sprawling out of the openings like drunkards passed out in a doorway. Large birds would swoop down and tear at the bags with determination. Stray papers and egg shells, broken cups and worn out toys would scatter every which way. No one wanted to pick up the debris, the nasty little crumbs of each other's lives.

Then, during a community picnic over the summer, Tim suggested they make their own trash pit. A grass-covered slope near the cul-de-sac would be the perfect spot. A common area intended as an emergency water overflow hold, the slope was already bowl-shaped. Delighted, the community citizens couldn't wait. They grabbed the nearest trash of chicken bones, paper plates, red cups, and popped balloons from a children's relay and lined up in a parade to march to the common area.

Without being told the community members knew what to do. They stood along the rim of the bowl and, one by one, threw their trash into their new pit. It worked. Nothing blew out or scattered in the street.

"What about the birds," asked Helen.

"I'll get a net from the store. Spread it across," said a man who lived across the street and two houses down.

Tim's wife seemed uncertain. "But I don't want anyone to see our pit."

Several of the community members nodded.

"Trees," suggested Helen. "We can plant trees along the rim."

And so it was decided. Helen priced trees at the store and brought back numbers to the group. After much debate, hands reached into pockets and purses and an amount was collected to purchase a net and one tree. Helen was disappointed. She'd imagined an impressive ring of oaks or birches with their silvery bark. With the community's money, she'd only be able to buy a regular old redbud.

Although disappointed, Helen took her task seriously and purchased the tree, marked down because it was fall. One of the neighbors dug a hole on the rim and then, with Helen's help, broke up the root ball and settled the tree into place. Helen watered the redbud to get it established. They'd need the tree's branches to provide privacy because the pile of trash had continued to grow.

All through the winter the people of the community brought their soup cans and take out containers, drink bottles and worn out shoes. In the spring the tree extended its branches. Leaves unfurled. Buds appeared. Helen had done a good job of watering it. And then, when it was time, the flowers budded. Whispers spread through the community and everyone came to see. The flowers were doll's heads, a wadded up test with a red "F", and little Jimmy's half-eaten hot dog from a month before.

Nervous laughter moved through the crowd.

"Its roots grew down into the pit," said Tim. "The tree is sucking up our trash."

No one had a solution, but the problem went away. Or, it became less important. The "flowers" eventually withered and fell back down into the pit. And, if there were uncomfortable moments such as when the tree bloomed the credit report of the Smiths, most of the trash was indistinguishable, one family from another.

And then the flowers stopped. The last tennis shoe on the end of the highest branch fell off and into the pit. The tree's trunk began to grow, to bulge. The children claimed they could hear gurgling sounds such as one would hear in a father's belly after a big meal.

The community called in a tree doctor. He came with a stethoscope and listened with a grave expression. He shook his head and said there was nothing he could do.

A month passed and a smell emanated from the deformed tree, a rotting, putrid smell. And then the bark split open and a thick black goo oozed down the trunk.

"It's got a blockage," said Helen. "It tried to suck up something too big."

The tree began to shake.

The people gathered around to watch the shaking tree, the oozing tree, the tree that smelled like gangrene. And then a black volcano erupted, blowing off the top branches. Black droplets of partially digested rubber rained on the people.

"A tire," said Tim. "It tried to suck up a tire."

The community members ducked and ran, trying to get away from the exploding tree, but the blockage was gone. Trash from the pit exploded from the top of the tree and rained down. Dirty diapers, mail order catalogues, raked leaves, and sour milk cartons.

The people hid in the nearest houses to the common area and stared in amazement. All the trash, everything so carefully held down by the net had been sucked up by the tree's roots and made its way out of the maple's ruined top. Trash, thick and wet, littered the yards, the pools, the streets. The tree, finished, lay split in half on the rim of the pit.

"I bought it half-price," said Helen in amazement.

"That's your fault then," said Tim, with a solemn nod. "Can't buy a half-price tree and expect it to do the job of a full-priced one."

MONSTERS BEAUTIFUL AND BRIGHT

The heart-clock ticked and then again. And a third time, but it was too slow. It wasn't enough.

Monsters Beautiful and Bright

*B*rigit cupped the bird in one hand and brought the line of feathers she'd made from colored scraps closer to the extended wing, cursing because this was a delicate operation. A witch needed a good pair of reading glasses if she was going to repair rot damage and damned if she knew where hers were. She squinted at the space where she'd cut the rot away and then pressed down on the top of the new feathers with her index finger, rubbing back and forth so the glue would dry evenly.

"There," she said. "Try it now."

The woodpecker—a handsome fellow as large as her arm with a bright red crest and dark gray body—straightened and extended his wings. The repaired wing didn't extend quite the same, but it had the benefit of the middle section being hot pink and teal now.

He squawked what Brigit decided to accept as a 'thank you.'

"I'll check the repair in the morning and then you can be on your way." She ushered him into a large bird crate. "Stay away from the rot next time."

Easier said than done. Ever since the demise of the three-headed goddess, rot had bloomed throughout the forest, eating holes in vegetation and animals alike. The priest for the new god blamed the people, demanded sacrifices, and suggested war as a way to revitalize the economy.

That's why Brigit lived out here, a hermit in a cottage. She scratched behind her ear and felt the distinct shape of her glasses.

"Ha." She removed them from the top of her head, plucking a hair out as she did. Faded red hair with an inch of gray at the root. She dropped the glasses inside her apron pocket and held the hair over a candle flame until it caught. No sense giving away power.

Time to clean up from the bird's repair. Buttons returned to their jars, needles stabbed into a pincushion, spools of thread sorted by thickness and then color. A board against the wall held pliers and wrenches and a box of things that might be useful in the future, including an antique pocket watch.

Outside the window a squawking erupted from the hedge that surrounded Brigit's cottage. The jays were no doubt being jerks again. But no, that was their warning cry.

Brigit looked out and gasped. People had advanced inside her hedge. This was no accident. The forest all around was filled with rot and Bruno wandered through it, allowing himself to be seen so as to keep visitors away. She was under attack. They'd sacrifice her to their god and then steal the food she'd grown through careful fight against rot. She may look older and helpless, but she wasn't giving in without a fight.

Grabbing her broom, Brigit threw open the door and stomped across her patio and down the path, her rubber boots making a squelching noise.

"How dare you come into my garden!" Brigit gripped the handle of her broom with both hands, and glared, even as she adjusted her initial assessment.

The intruders stood at the bird feeders gobbling the squares of yellow, red, and purple fruit she'd cut early this morning. The girl looked to be about sixteen, taller than Brigit. Juice ran down her chin in sticky rivulets. Next to her, the boy was younger and wore pants with holes in the knees and a scared expression. He thrust his hands, full of crushed fruit, behind his back as if to hide his thievery.

"It's the witch." The girl pivoted toward the forest. "Run, Gregor!"

Before he could, Jay Junior popped from the bushes and flew at the boy, divebombing again and again. The boy, Gregor, covered his head with his arms. Brigit didn't blame him. JJ's beak was made of silver and very sharp. She kept meaning to file the tip.

"Stay away from us." The girl waved her arms in the air. "You monsters!"

JJ screeched for help and other birds emerged from the tree tops. Movement at the forest's tree line told Brigit that Bruno was nearby, lurking, watching to make sure she was okay. This was going to get nasty if she didn't intervene.

"Enough," Brigit yelled. She grabbed Gregor's arm with one hand, dragging him toward the cottage.

"Let go of my brother," the girl grabbed onto Brigit, plucking at her fingers. "I won't let you eat us or turn us into monsters."

Brigit stumbled, only the broom in her hand keeping her from falling on her face.

A low growling came from the forest a moment before a large wolf sprinted toward the hedge, clearing the vegetation, his silver leg shining.

Brigit pushed the two forward into the cottage and pulled the door shut behind her.

Gregor was shaking, but the girl was trying to get away and Brigit had neither the time nor the energy for this nonsense. She used the broom handle to shepherd them past the worktable to the kitchen.

"Sit."

Gregor sat, eyes wide as he stared at her. The girl looked around the cottage, but Brigit was standing between her and the door. She sat down.

Brigit put her hands on her hips. Something wasn't adding up. These two didn't look like soldiers, not with juice dripping down their faces, but they did look half-starved.

Then she turned the boy around and said, "Who are you? Who else is in the woods?"

The boy shrank away, lifting his hands as if she were going to hit him.

"If you hurt him…you'll be sorry." The girl didn't seem to know how to finish so she tapped her foot and then regathered steam. "We didn't do anything to you. Now let us go."

"You came through the gate onto my property, ate my food, and assaulted my animals." Brigit scowled. "You've done quite enough."

"We got lost and then something was chasing us. When we saw your house, we were hungry and we needed to eat."

Maybe that was true and maybe it wasn't.

Brigit paced from the kitchen on one side of the house, past the table with the teenagers, to the craft table. More people wandering the woods meant that her cottage was exposed. She'd been fighting rot in the Borderlands for a long time, doing what she could to save the animals. If people came here then they'd kill her animals because they were 'unnatural.' But, if these siblings were lost, then she had to figure out a way to get them back to the village.

The wood pecker in his cage lifted his wings, annoyed at all the fuss. Brigit opened the cage and let him step out onto her arm. "I am a witch and this is one of my monsters."

Nodding with a self-satisfied air, the girl crossed her arms over her chest.

"He can tell when people are lying and then he'll squawk. Do you understand?" This wasn't true at all, but she might as well lean into whatever the villagers said about her.

The girl tilted her head. "So he'll squawk if you lie too?"

Teenagers. They picked everything apart.

"I'm a person so the rule pertains to me as well." She sat down in the empty chair. "There will be a group of villagers looking for you by now."

"No one will look for us." There was a dark tone to the way the girl said this that marked it as truth.

"What's your name?"

"Ha! I know enough not to tell you. Then you'll have power over me."

Brigit prayed to the dead goddess for patience. "I'm not going to hurt you."

The siblings looked at the bird, but he didn't squawk.

Gregor made a fist with his thumb on the outside and made a circle on his chest. Then his hands moved together and he pointed to his head.

"No," the girl said to Gregor. "She's not nice. She deserves to be burned on a pyre as a sacrifice for Camulus."

Brigit cocked her head and thought of a thousand sarcastic things to say, but went with, "Say that name in my house again and I'll feed you to the wolf."

Gregor made rapid motions with his hands.

"She wouldn't dare let it in," the girl whispered to Gregor. "The monster would eat her too."

"Why doesn't Gregor talk?" Brigit asked, trying to fight her curiosity. It was obvious these children had been through a lot, but she had to stay impersonal and return them to the village. The last time she'd cared she'd watched the goddess's dragon heads be chopped off, one by one, and then the sacred body thrown into the sea. Staying in this little area of the woods and fighting rot were all Brigit had left.

"None of your business."

They all looked at the woodpecker; he rubbed his beak at the bright new feathers with a satisfied air. Brigit sighed. It was so hard to depend on birds for help.

"Fine." She stood up and pulled out two quilts from the hall closet behind Gregor's chair. "I'll show you where you can sleep." She led the way to the backroom where the walls were lined with canned goods and jellies.

The floor was clean, she swept it every day, and the blankets would keep them warm. This was better than if they'd slept out in the woods.

"You're safe as long as you're in here," Brigit said. Then she shut the door to the back room like she'd pull a cover over a bird's cage and went to bed.

Tired from a night of sleep disturbed by wondering how she was going to get her unwanted guests home, Brigit opened the door to the back room.

"I'm going to make breakfast. Would you like some?"

Gregor nodded an eager yes, but the girl, who was stretching her arms overhead, dropped her arms and shook her head. "You're trying to fatten us up so you can eat us."

Brigit laughed until she started coughing and had to catch her breath. "Is that what they say about me in the village?"

A clicking sound made all three look at the door. Then giant paws thudded against the door, making the glass rattle. One paw was silver, the other was fur. The wolf's nose pressed against the door creating an oval of condensation.

The girl whimpered and pressed against the back of her cage.

Brigit walked toward the door. "Hold your horses, Bruno, I'm coming."

"Please, I'll do anything. Don't open the door."

Brigit touched the doorknob. "What's your name?"

"Hannah." The girl's voice was high-pitched with fear.

"Someone outside needs my help. Please be brave. I promise Bruno won't hurt you." She waited for Gregor's short nod and Hannah's more grudging one before opening the door.

The wolf trotted to the work table, reared up and opened his mouth. A squirrel fell out and laid in a limp pile of red-brown fur. The body seemed fine, but the tail had rot.

Brigit felt a wave a fury and pity. Poor thing. An innocent victim in this power struggle between deities and humans. "What do we have here?" She stroked the wolf's head, scratching behind Bruno's ears. She began to hum as she went into the arts and crafts room and selected several supplies.

First, she used a razor to shave off the fur remaining on the tail. Then she put on gloves and squeezed the tail until moisture oozed out of it. A putrid odor filled the air and Hannah coughed from the back room. Next, Brigit wiped her hands on her apron and squeezed a moulding clay into her dry hands. She rubbed back and forth to warm the material and then smoothed it around the squirrel's tail so that whole thing was thicker, the tailbone entirely encased. Using water, Brigit smoothed the clay and then went to a stack of tiny drawers and pulled out what looked like green doll hair. She measured the hair to the tail, snipped, and then began pressing chunks into the clay.

"I can't see," Hannah called.

Lost in the work, Brigit looked up, confused. Then she shifted to the side so Hannah and Gregor had a better view. When the tail was covered, Brigit carried the squirrel over to a spot of sunlight and carefully arranged its limbs.

"Well," she said, putting her hands on her back and stretching. "That's a way to start the morning."

The wolf whined and Brigit laughed before disappearing into the kitchen. She reappeared a moment later with a bowl of water and set in on the floor. "Good work, Bruno."

Hannah pressed against the bars. "Why are you doing that if you're going to eat it?"

Brigit opened the woodpecker's cage and tapped the repaired wing. "Why in the world would I eat the squirrel?" She looked at the wolf. "Bruno might, but not today. He's a carnivore after all. Not much I can do about that." Then Brigit hefted the bird cage and opened the door to outside. The woodpecker launched himself into the air and Brigit smiled, wishing him good flight.

"But," Hannah looked at Gregor, who shrugged his shoulders. "If you're not going to eat us and you're not going to feed us to the wolf, why did you lock us in that cellar?"

Brigit gave them a stern look. "Because I have many things, magical or not, that I don't want children to get into while I'm not around."

Hannah swallowed. "That makes sense. We don't know you and you don't know us."

"You can be my guests." Brigit held up a finger, "But, if you try to attack me or escape, I'll send Bruno after you."

Hannah nodded acceptance.

Brigit brought out plates of fruit and muffins with fruit baked inside. They were delicious, if she did say so. Judging by the speed with which the muffins disappeared, the siblings agreed.

Hannah closed her eyes as she enjoyed each bite. "We haven't had anything this good in so long."

"How long were you lost?"

"Only a day," Hannah said. "But we're on rations back home. Mother had to go to Camulus's temple for our share."

Brigit's mind spun. Both children dirty and starving though they'd only been lost a day. Gregor shrinking away as if she would hit him. "And your father?"

"He died in the war. That's when Gregor stopped talking. He can, you know, but he doesn't."

"Here, boy, eat another muffin." Brigit's voice came out gruff. "You're nothing but skin and bones."

"Thank you," Hannah said for Gregor.

"How do I say 'you're welcome'?" Brigit said.

Gregor and Hannah looked at each other and then Gregor made a motion.

Brigit mimicked it and then stood up. "Now, taking care of you has put me behind in today's chores. I'll need your help to catch up and then I'll lead you back to the village."

Gregor nodded his head, but Hannah stood and stacked the plates and wouldn't meet Brigit's eyes.

The trees needed to be scrubbed today. Brigit hummed as she gathered the chisels, a bucket, and a broom.

Standing by the sink, Hannah rinsed the last plate in soapy water. "Can we stay one more night? Please?"

Gregor grabbed Hannah's arm and used his other hand to touch his chin and then pantomimed stroking long hair.

Brigit didn't need Hannah to tell her that Gregor wanted his mother. She rapped her knuckles against the work table. "I'm very sorry, dearie, but I like living alone." To change the topic, Brigit motioned Hannah closer and touched the squirrel's tail. "See how it's dry now?"

Hannah pet the green hair. It was fluffy and sprang back into place. "Why did you use green?"

"It'll blend in with the leaves. Camouflage. Also, it's pretty. Don't you think?"

Hannah nodded and smiled.

"Here's the magic part." Brigit leaned forward over the animal and blew like she was blowing through a straw right into the squirrel's face. Its bright, black eyes opened and it jumped to its feet, paws dangling and nose sniffing.

Brigit opened a window and the little squirrel hopped out and into the apple tree. "There we go," she said with satisfaction. "It's the love that wakes them up."

"Your magic is kinda like what I did with my toy back home when all the stuffing came out," Hannah said, marvelling. "Will you teach me how to do this magic?"

If no one was looking for the siblings, then there wasn't such a rush. Having some extra hands would be a real help. Maybe another day wouldn't hurt.

"Magic," Brigit said, "is an easy word for what is mostly hard work."

The siblings watched while Brigit showed them how to inspect the trees around the cottage.

"See the bark peeling up here?" Brigit pulled at the loose bark to reveal a dark gray ash, the first sign of rot. Later it would turn into a black tar and stick to whatever it touched, burning through bark, wing, or skin.

Gregor made frantic gestures to Hannah.

Brigit tried to figure them out, but Hannah interpreted. "We can't get near rot. It'll kill us. That's why we have to keep moving inland. That's why we have to attack the east. So we won't run out of land."

"Not true. We can take care of our own land. We just need gloves. And we have to burn the infected pieces." Brigit sighed. "Look, gods and goddesses are selfish and they're served by selfish humans. Everyone in power wants to help themselves. Camulus is a war god. More war equals more power for him."

"He made the rot?" Hannah's eyes were huge. "But, the rot has always been around. It's…real." She shook her head. "We learn about it in school."

"The rot didn't come until the Morrigan was killed by Camulus. Our land reflects our leaders."

"What's the Morrigan?"

Brigit put on gloves and moved to a tree. She used a chisel to scrap the rotted section into the bucket. "A goddess with three parts: Badb, Macha, and Nemain. Each goddess had an affinity for plants, for animals, for children. Together, they confer sovereignty and that creates a bond with the land between spirit, human, and nature." Brigit dipped the chisel into spackle to spread a nurturing paste over the bare spot. "This'll keep bugs and new rot away. Then we breathe a blessing on the repair and give a little love." Brigit patted the tree.

"I wish that the Morrigan was still in charge," Hannah said, picking at a blade of grass. "Is there a way to bring her back?"

"It's not all about gods and goddesses and who is in charge. It's what we humans decide to do about it." Brigit winked. "Besides, goddesses can be difficult to keep dead."

Hannah looked at Gregor and took a deep breath. Then she put on a glove and used the chisel to pull up a piece of bark. Once he saw his sister working, Gregor joined in.

Brigit went inside to make lemonade and watched through the window. The kids were a little awkward—Gregor had his tongue between his teeth as he used the chisel—but they were taking it seriously. She went outside and handed him a drink, told him to take a break. Then she went over to Hannah.

They sat in the shade and watched while Bruno went up to Gregor. The boy held out a hand. Bruno sniffed it and Gregor smiled.

Then Bruno huffed and lay down beside Gregor. Scared, Gregor looked to Hannah, who looked to Brigit.

"Scratch behind his ears. He loves that."

They watched in silence as Gregor scratched and Bruno closed his eyes in pleasure.

Hannah picked at a piece of grass. "You're not what I thought a witch would be."

"Hm." Brigit spread out on the grass and moved her rubber boots back and forth. "What did you think I would be like?"

Shaking her head, Hannah whispered, "I don't know." Then she took a deep breath. "They told us the Borderlands are dangerous. That the rot will kill us. That witches and monsters live here."

"All true." Brigit watched her monster roll onto his back so that the boy could rub his belly.

"But, it was my step-father who brought us here." Her voice hitched. "On purpose. While my mother was away. He told us not to come back. That he would tell my mother we'd been killed by the monsters in the forest."

Brigit tried to keep herself calm, but the same instinct that made her protect the animals was waking inside.

"My mother said he'd be able to take care of us, protect us. Because he's one of the the high priests for Camulus."

Chills swept over Brigit and she had to look up at the leaves in the tree so Hannah wouldn't see her expression. "Of course he is," she murmured. Witches are attuned to the music strings of the universe, but this wasn't a gentle whisper. This was claws against strings. And she got to be a part of whatever was happening. Terrifying and thrilling.

"But." Hannah turned away, but Brigit could still hear. "He can be really mean to us."

"I believe you," Brigit said, voice low so that Gregor wouldn't hear, but with enough conviction that Hannah would feel it. "You don't have to prove it to me or show me the scars. I believe you."

Hannah stayed turned around and Brigit touched her shoulder and then stood up to give her privacy. It was getting dark. Too dangerous to travel through the Borderlands even with Bruno. A small voice of reason inside tried to argue, but she squelched it. These children needed her help.

"Alright, I need everyone over here for this part."

Gregor and Hannah, who'd wiped her face on her sleeve, came over. Brigit used her broom to sweep a clear area off to the side of the porch. Then she set the bucket of contaminated rot in the middle and set it on fire.

"Fire, fire burning bright, light the darkness of the night." Brigit chanted the words and then Hannah and Gregor began to dance in the dusk, adding their voices to hers. When the rot was burned, Brigit added a packet of sage on top to cleanse the air.

Pleased with the day, maybe even a little reckless, Brigit called Hannah over to the tree they'd scraped earlier.

"Take those feelings you have inside, the positive ones, and then rub the tree. You'll be able to call forth new bark."

"I can't touch it without gloves."

"You can," Brigit said, placing her own hand on the tree. She allowed her love for the tree to flow from her, humming as she encouraged the tree to trust her, to try again. Little patches of roughness formed, she imagined like scabs on a wound. Brigit stepped back. "Your turn."

Hannah placed her shaking hand where Brigit's had been. "Grow," she said, but she was already pulling her hand away so that only her fingertips touched. "Grow." Pulling her hand away, Hannah shook her head. "It doesn't work. You have to be born a witch."

Disappointed, Brigit said, "It was too soon. You can't forget your fear of rot in one day." She looked out into the evening at the way the light touched all of the trees and flowers that she knew so well. "The trick, though, is to think less about what's making you afraid and more about what you love."

With a lazy lope, Bruno disappeared into the woods for dinner and they went inside for their own. Afterwards, looking tired, Hannah started toward the back room.

"I guess you two can sleep in the spare bedroom. But I'm taking you home first thing in the morning." It was as much an admonition to the children as to herself. She was growing too fond of them.

The spare bedroom had two beds. Right after Hannah climbed into hers, Bruno howled from outside, his metal paw clicking against the glass. Brigit straightened from tucking the girl in and ran to the bedroom door. "There's another rescue tonight."

Together, they rushed down the stairs.

Brigit lifted the candle and saw a human form draped across the wolf's back. Someone else lost in the Borderlands. When the wolf came in through the door, Hannah clutched her chest. "Mom!"

Tearstains marked a path through the dirt on the woman's face. Blood on her arms suggested struggling through brambles. Ripped clothing and no shoes suggested haste. Fleeing from danger into danger.

"Help me get her to the work table." Brigit supported her head and the children hefted her slight body up.

Foreboding made Brigit's hands clumsy as she searched for a heartbeat. Nothing there. She rolled up the woman's sleeves and saw the fresh bruises. A fight. After the children had been "lost." Brigit shook her head. "I'm so sorry, children. Your mother has died of a broken heart."

"You can fix this," Hannah said, her voice high like a young child's. "You fix the rot and the squirrel and the trees."

Brigit licked her dry lips. "This isn't the same."

"Please," Hannah begged. "Please try." A wavy image of a decapitated dragon head appeared in the air above Hannah and then disappeared when Brigit blinked her eyes.

Power was in the room tonight.

Brigit swallowed and then looked at the work bench. How does one make a heart? Metal like a wolf's paw? Satin scraps like a bird's wing? The pocket watch. It had waited for a use for years. Now it was, quite literally, time.

"I can't," Brigit said, "but I can help you to do it."

"I'm not ready." Hannah's eyes widened. "This is too important to mess up."

"You told me about fixing your toy. This is the same. Everything you need is over there." She nodded at the art supplies, the crafting materials, the hand tools. "Remember, magic is an easy word for what is mostly hard work. Think about what you love, not what you fear."

"Yes, I can do it." Hannah calmed and nodded her head. "Gregor, you need to help me."

The three worked through the night: cutting, sewing, using candle wax as glue. Every bit had a memory and Brigit made Hannah hold the materials as she described her mother singing at bedtime, promising that things would get better, standing in line for hours to get food for the family. When Gregor cried, Brigit held the cotton to his face to absorb his tears and then gave it back to Hannah.

When they were finished, they had a heart with the pocket watch as the center. Encasing it was a satin flower petal—purple because Mother loved purple and a flower to represent beauty. Cotton padding because Mother was soft. A smooth stone painted with three stick figures because Mother was strong, too. A piece of elastic because Brigit said every heart should have room to grow. Everything sewn by the hand.

"Last step," Brigit said. She was scared this wouldn't work, that Gregor and Hannah's hearts were now in danger of breaking. All six hands placed the chain around Mother's neck so that the new heart settled outside of the broken one.

Brigit made the sacrifice. "You're safe here," she said. "With your children. You can stay. You can all stay."

The heart-clock ticked and then again. And a third time, but it was too slow. It wasn't enough.

"I love you." Hannah sniffled back her tears. "Please, Mama. You've found us."

Gregor nudged Hannah away and looked into his mother's face. "Mom," he said. His voice was rusty, unused, but the words were clear. "Come home."

Ticking marked the seconds passing.

Brigit narrowed her eyes. It seemed like the heart was settling more deeply, but maybe that was wishful thinking.

"Ah," Hannah straightened. "I understand." She held Gregor's hand and her mother's, but looked at Brigit. "Thank you for the invitation to stay, but I can't. I need to go and tell other villages about the rot. That magic is hard work, but I can teach them."

Brigit nodded, admiration shining through her. Hannah made the heart, Hannah had to make the sacrifice. "I'll keep your mother and brother safe until you return."

Mother's eyes fluttered open. Her hand went to the watch-flower-cotton-rock on her chest. She sat up and opened her arms wide.

Bruno howled, his animal instincts overcome by the emotion in the cottage. Brigit's chin wobbled with the same.

Hannah and Gregor climbed on the work table to envelop their mother in a hug, Hannah pulling Brigit in a moment later and Bruno put his mismatched paws up so he could shove his nose into the mess of human bodies.

The morning sun shined in through the window and the hug released. The faint, steady ticking of Mother's new heart filled the silence. Gregor made circles with his thumb and index and rotated them.

"Family." Hannah let out a shaky breath. "Couldn't have said it better."

The Boy from Omran

*T*he first time it rains at the new house water soaks the basement carpet, water that smells dark and secret like the ocean. Identical twins Jane and Alice stand on either side of the damp stain and watch the water in the middle gurgle up from underneath the carpet like a baking soda volcano from their school science fair. Then the water recedes with a sound like a bathtub draining. The girls are seven years old. Jane wears shorts and Alice wears dresses, Jane likes to climb trees and Alice decorates cupcakes, Jane is feisty and talks back while Alice simpers and smiles. Each morning the twins decide who will be Jane and who will be Alice.

"We'll need to replace the door," their mother says. She makes a face as the water squelches between her toes. Mother sells vacuum cleaners, but even the model 3200 would have trouble sucking up this much water. She'll need to borrow an extractor and carpet blowers from the main office.

"That's where the water is getting in," Dad agrees. "This house is our personal money pit."

He and Mother had bought the house in the country, but not near the golf courses that Dad managed. They couldn't afford that. Instead, the run-down house sat under scraggly trees, far from sidewalks and sunlight, and now the school bus would come a half

111

hour earlier in the mornings. Dad said this would keep them out of trouble.

Mother and Dad go upstairs, but the twins stare at the puddle. It is clear to them that the water isn't rain, isn't coming from the door, and isn't stopping. Without needing to discuss it, the girls go to the attic to fetch their older brother, Peter.

Peter leads the way back to the basement, not because he believes the girls but because he is bored. Peter is in middle school and wears the typical uniform: athletic shorts, t-shirt, and socks the color of one's favorite sports team, in his case, the Pittsburgh Steelers.

"Ewww, it's really gross." Unbeknownst to Peter, his disgusted facial expression is similar to the one his mother made earlier.

"We told you." Jane puts her hands on her hips.

Peter kneels on the carpet in front of the fountain. "Why'd the parental units say the water was coming from the door?"

Alice shrugs. "Adults like to complicate things."

"Well, I'll make it simple." He pulls out his Swiss Army knife, a present when he turned ten, and selects a serrated edge. He cuts the carpet with two strokes and pulls up the resulting corner to expose warped wood with a handle. A dank smell of mildew makes Alice sneeze.

"It's a trap door." Now Peter sounds excited.

"To what?" Jane demands. "Our backyard?"

"Maybe a root cellar." Peter seizes the handle and strains. The twins get behind him and hold onto his waist for extra leverage.

The hatch opens with a wet sucking noise. The water around the edge of the hatch drains back down and the three bend over to look into the darkness. A wave of cold washes up and over them followed by the mineral smell of wet rock.

Then, from the cold, a boy's head pops out of the hole up to his shoulders. He has a riot of wet dark curls, large limpid eyes set in a brown face, and looks about the twins' age. His mouth gapes open as he sucks in air.

"Who are you?" they all ask, the boy included.

He answers first, English clear but accented. "Khalil."

"Where did you come from?" today's Alice asks delicately. She sees the dirt on his face and the way his collarbone juts out of the skin and thinks that he has been hungry for a long time.

"From Omran, across the ocean." Khalil stands up straighter, taking pride in his homeland, and then gestures down into the hole. The children hear a faint sound that might be an echo of waves slapping against rock. "And then into this cave. But then the water started to rise higher and higher until I was floating against that piece of wood. I kept my foot against a piece of rock so I could press my face to the wood. I inhaled each time the waves went out, but I'm so tired." He taps the trap door. "I almost drowned."

"She means," says Jane, "why are you in our basement?"

"I'm not in anyone's basement." Khalil's shoulders straighten with indignation. "I'm waiting for my mother to call, but the phone ran out of battery because I've been waiting ever so long. It's hard to tell time in a dark cave." He holds up a cell phone in a baggie as proof.

Alice accepts the phone and passes it to Peter.

"It looks like a toy," Jane says.

"It isn't a toy," says Peter with the authority of a middle schooler. He takes it out of the baggie and turns it over and over in his hands. "But it is different. A flip-top." He runs a thumb over the port. "Maybe one of Dad's old chargers will fit. Come on out and we'll try it."

"No," Khalil says. "I can't leave. My mother is holding back the monsters. She won't know where I've gone."

"What monsters?" Alice grabs for Jane's hand. They scoot closer to the hole. It is possible to hear claws scrape against rock as if a lizard moved in the darkness.

Peter sets the phone on a nearby table and moves the twins aside. "Look guys, there's no ocean around here." He kneels down and reaches his arm past Khalil's torso. It definitely feels like the side of a cave, the rocks sharp enough to dig into his hand. "Maybe an underground spring?" He pulls out the mini-flashlight on his Swiss Army knife. "I'm going to check it out."

"The monsters are horrible," says Khalil, moving to the side of the opening so Peter can climb down, but otherwise ignoring Peter's explorations. "Ghuls. Bigger than me with arms that end in dirty claws. Their eyes are sewed shut, but their mouths are always open with sharp teeth. If they bite you, you turn into a monster too, but if you cut them open then maggots fall out."

Alice shudders and even Jane swallows a nervous moan. "Why are the monsters chasing you?"

Khalil's dark eyes meet Alice's. "Don't know. They attacked our village in the middle of the night. My mom and I got in a boat, but they chased us across the ocean, biting and snapping until our boat split in half. My mother held the sides together and I paddled as fast as I could. She called to the wind to blow us farther away from the monsters. Then we saw the cave. We thought we'd be safe, but the monsters came again." He sighed. "I haven't seen any of the other families from our village."

"This cave goes on and on," Peter calls from the blackness. "How can it be underneath our house in the woods?"

"Then what happened?" Alice asks.

"My mother gave me the paddle to use as a float. She let go of the pieces of the boat and we both swam for the cave. The monsters don't see very well. I kicked and kicked my feet until I was in the cave and I crawled up onto the rocks. I wanted to use the paddle to hit the monsters, but my mother said not to. She spread across the opening, reaching her fingers up and up and up to the top and her toes down and down and down to the water. The wind pulled at her dress and it stretched like a boat's sail until the moonlight was blocked, the water muted, and the monsters kept out. Over the wind, I heard her tell me to go, that she would hold them back and then come to me when it was safe."

"You mom is really brave," Alice says.

"Our mom sells vacuum cleaners," says Jane.

"Kids, dinner." Their mother's voice drifts down the stairs.

Peter pulls himself out through the trapdoor. "Looks like the water is receding for good. Do you want to come out and go to dinner with us?"

Khalil looks around the room, the labeled cardboard boxes that still haven't been unpacked since the move, the noisy fans by the door, the overhead lights beating down. It is all different than Omran and he can't imagine himself in this place. It is too foreign, too strange. He is familiar with the feel of the cave and the sound of monsters and the hope of his mother, but he doesn't know how to explain all these things so he just shakes his head.

Peter nods. "We'll come back later. And bring you food."

Khalil backs down the hole and perches on part of the rock wall. The water doesn't reach his feet. Peter shuts the wooden door and flips the wet carpet back into place.

Food is already on the table: overcooked chicken breast, lumpy brown gravy, green beans, and rice.

"You forgot my place again," says Peter. He is annoyed. Ever since they moved here, he attends a private school during the week and comes home on the weekends.

"Get yourself a plate and sit down for grace," Dad says. When they've all bowed their heads, he says, "Let us look with eyes that see, feel with soft hearts, and give as we have been given. Amen."

The bowls of food are passed around counter-clockwise.

"Jane, fix your hair, please. It's hanging in your face," says Mother.

"I'm Alice," says today's Alice. She smoothes her hair as, across the table, Jane shoves a napkin full of food into her pocket to give to Khalil later.

"Really?" Mother frowns at today's Alice. "I thought Jane had the little beauty mark."

Alice sighs. "Jane is the adventurous one. She wears shorts and talks back."

Dad snaps open a newspaper and holds it in front of his plate like a privacy screen.

"Football tryouts are next week," says Peter. "Have you signed the release?"

The whole house lurches, shaking from the foundation up to the attic. Windows rattle and lights flicker. Wind rushes through the kitchen and Peter smells the mineral scent of wet rocks.

"It's the monsters," says Alice. Her lower lip trembles.

"There's no such thing as monsters," Mother says, pointing her fork at Alice. "That's the house settling. We'll probably have to replace the windows before winter." She sighs. "There goes the bonus I earned this month."

"There are too monsters," blurts Jane. "In our basement."

The house quiets and all is still. Dad's newspaper crinkles as he gives it a shake. "I don't want any of you going down into the basement until we've fixed the leak."

115

So they have to wait until almost midnight before the blue light and laugh track from the television in their parents' bedroom goes off. At least there was time for Khalil's flip phone to charge with an old charger at the back of the odds and ends drawer. Peter has his mini flashlight out and leads the way. Alice, thinking the middle spot is the safest, tells Jane, "You go behind me."

"No, I don't want to." Jane adjusts a stuffed yellow and pink owl under her arm.

"You have to. Jane is the brave, adventurous one."

Jane shakes her head. "I don't want to be Jane anymore."

"Too bad."

As they descend the basement stairs, the reek of seawater and rock grows stronger. They work quickly to pull back the carpet and lift the wooden trap door. Khalil is waiting and takes the food from Jane, shoving it into his mouth as if the chicken weren't dried out and the green beans squished from being rolled in the napkin.

Peter has been thinking about the water. About how something was holding the water back and now isn't. About how the monsters are coming. He thinks Khalil's mother is dead, but he doesn't know if Khalil has figured this out yet. "Here's your phone," he says when Khalil finishes wiping crumbs on his pants.

The hope on Khalil's face as the phone rings is a terrible thing and Peter looks away. They can all hear a woman's voice in what is both a foreign language and clearly a recorded voice message. Khalil flips the phone closed. "She didn't pick up."

Peter clears his throat so he has time to think. "You need to come with us."

"No, I can't. I won't leave her. You don't understand. She'll come for me." He takes a step back into the darkness.

Jane says, "You can't wait. Go find her."

Khalil gives a single nod. His lips are pressed tight. Below him comes that terrible clattering sound of claws against rock.

Peter holds out his Swiss Army knife. In a gruff voice he says, "You can use the light by twisting. And there's a sharp blade, if you need it."

Jane offers her stuffed owl. "Just for tonight. We'll be back in the morning and you can return it then." She wants to give him an excuse to take it without blubbering or looking like a baby.

"That was a very Alice thing to do," Alice says with approval.

The next morning the twins have an argument over who will be Jane and who will be Alice.

"We need a strong Jane, someone brave who can help Khalil today."

"Being Alice is important today too. We need her to be sensitive." Last night, as they walked back to their bedrooms, Peter had explained his reasons for thinking that Khalil's mother was dead and then Jane had felt bad that she'd told him to go find his mother.

"Well," says one twin doubtfully, "I'm not sure I'm brave or sensitive enough."

"Me neither."

While they both consider this problem, a mechanical whining interspersed with pounding comes clear. Peter runs past their room and shouts, "Come on." They hear his footsteps crashing down the basement steps.

"I think we'll both have to be brave. Maybe Jane can be brave and sensitive and Alice can be sensitive and brave."

With a nod the twins dress themselves in matching one-piece rompers—one coral and one turquoise. They run down to the basement.

The entire level is an anthill of activity. One man walks by with a two by four over his shoulder. Sawdust filters through the air. The door to the outside has been removed and the glimpse of trees is disconcerting. The insistent whine of a miter saw makes it hard to think. In all the confusion it takes Peter a moment to figure out what the men wearing the t-shirts of a local company are doing. They are cutting and spacing thick blocks on top of the wet carpet at intervals and cutting boards to make a new floor inches above the old one. They are sealing the entrance to Khalil's cave.

"Mother," Peter shouts.

Mother waves. She is wearing a construction hat. "We're renovating the basement. There's cereal and milk for breakfast," she shouts back.

The sawdust makes Alice's eyes water.

"Stop it," shouts Jane.

Alice drops to the carpet and tries to pry up the boards covering Khalil's trap door, but the grooves of one beam fit into the next one and it's too hard for her.

Dad wanders around from work bench to work bench, nodding his head as if he were in charge. Peter feels a flash of anger and grabs Dad's arm. "You can't just cover it up."

Dad motions the nearest man to stop the saw so he can hear. "What's that, son?"

Peter turns in a circle to encompass the whole basement. "You can't build a new floor on top of soaked carpet. Mold will grow and it will move up the walls and throughout the house."

"Nonsense." Mother joins them. "We're very lucky that these men were willing to come out to work on a Sunday." She puts her hand on Dad's arm. "There are sprays for mold. No need to worry. We're adding value to our house. No one would want it the way it is: with a leak."

Dad nods to the construction man and the saw starts up again. Peter shakes his head and pulls Alice off the floor. Jane follows Mother outside, away from the noise of the saw, and puts her hands on her hips. She takes a deep breath and tells the truth. "There's a boy and he needs help. Monsters attacked his village and now they've killed his mother. He's underneath our basement and the construction is locking him in with the monsters."

Maybe Mother should have laughed sooner because in the instant after Jane stops speaking, the children see Mother's eyes shift to the right, her hands clench and release, and hear the false note in the laughter when it does erupt. "There are no monsters, no emergency, and certainly no boy in the basement," she gasps. "Don't your father and I have enough to do here with our house? Fixing the leak, replacing the windows, and I'd like to repaint the kitchen cabinets."

"You can redecorate your house all you want, but this is an emergency," Jane shouts. "I'll show you the trap door. It's right there." But, the new boards cover the door and Jane can see that Mother doesn't want to really look, the kind of looking that means moving things.

"Let's say there is a boy under our basement. And monsters. First, the boy is probably a monster too. Second, if you let one in, you're breaking the seal and letting them all in. Why would you let them infest our house? I say send them back to Omran where they came from. Everything is fine the way it is." Mother's chest rises and falls as she pants. "I have real problems without looking for more. Now, go play."

The children stay outside while Mother puts the ridiculous yellow hat back on and steps through the open doorway.

The children are all thinking the same thing, but Jane needs to say it out loud. "I never said Khalil was from Omran."

Alice feels betrayed. Her mother knew about the ghuls and the children like Khalil and kept it a secret.

Construction crews take lunch. Peter knows this to be a fact. So he and the twins walk around the side of the house where they can see the driveway.

"Why is she lying?" Jane asks. She is hurt and can't keep the quaver out of her voice.

"She doesn't want to see, so she doesn't." Peter is bitter, knowing that he will be an adult soon, but vowing that he will be different.

"The monsters are going to get Khalil," says Alice, wringing her hands.

"We'll help him," says Peter.

Alice is about to cry. "How?"

"We're going into the cave," says Jane.

The construction crew pile into their logoed white van and drive toward town. Then Mother and Dad come out and walk toward their car. He puts an arm around her and the children overhear him say, "You'll be safe by this evening."

The kids slip into the basement and begin dismantling the floor boards. It is similar to when they play with their Lincoln logs. Peter pulls back the carpet and they lift the trap door. Khalil doesn't pop out. The reptile smell from the hole is even worse. Jane knows that it is the monster smell, but she hopes Alice won't know that.

Peter goes first. The twins hold hands and follow. The rocks are slippery and it is dark. Darker than a bedroom with no nightlight.

"What if they come back and lock us in?" Alice says.

"We'll have to hurry." But Jane's heart beats a countdown. She should have insisted on being Alice today. It would feel good to whimper.

"There," whispers Peter. "I see something." A speck of light in the distance. Maybe from a mini flashlight.

They make their way through the darkness, their gaze on the light. It doesn't get much bigger, but now the children have to cover their noses with their arms to breathe through the rotten monster smell. Skittering sounds come from overhead. The monsters are crawling on the rock ceiling, the suction cups on their limbs giving away their position.

"Khalil?" Peter calls.

The light walks toward them and they see Khalil's face. He has the stuffed owl and his toy-like flip top phone. His eyes are sunken and he looks younger than before. "I walked all the way to the cave entrance. Mother is gone." He pulls out a piece of black cloth from a pocket of his dirty pants. "I found a scrap of her dress. She would never have taken it off. They ate my mother and turned her into a monster."

Peter nods. The children step around Khalil like an entourage, letting him feel safe in the middle. In the faint light they see the ghuls. Like gray salamanders, they slither through the darkness on the floor, on the ceiling, it makes no difference. Like Khalil described, their eyes are sewn shut. The children are surrounded.

"Don't run," says Jane. "Whatever we do, we mustn't run."

Alice lets out a tiny cry. "But, we have to hurry. The workers will be back from lunch. We'll be locked in."

Khalil hands Peter the flashlight so he can take Alice's hand.

"Let's go," says Peter. His voice trembles, but he moves first through the breathing darkness. His shoulders hunch as he expects a monster to fall on him at each step.

"Why are they waiting?" whispers Jane as they creep forward.

Up ahead they can see a dim light coming through the trap door. And then the largest monster hisses from the darkness. It moves forward to block their way out. Unlike the others, this one is black, the same shade as the scrap of cloth in Khalil's hand. The monster opens its mouth and saliva runs down its needle sharp teeth. The stitches on the eyes look new, a thread hanging inches past the knot on the end.

Peter straightens. Monsters lurk in the dark, in the fear, in the unknown. Peter lifts the mini flashlight and points it right at the monster's face. The monster hisses and ducks back into the shadows. Peter nods. He knows what he must do. "Go," he says to the younger children. "I'll hold him back with my light."

"No," cries Alice. "That's what Khahil's mother did. And she's dead."

Peter's hand tightens on the flashlight. He doesn't want to be lost in the dark, he doesn't want to be left in the cave, he doesn't want the monsters to bite him.

"Give me the light," Khalil says. His eyes are dark, but his voice is steadfast. "You can trust me."

Peter's hand shakes as he hands over the light. Then he feels like he can almost sense the beam of light shooting from the flashlight in Khalil's hand and spearing over his head into the darkness. When Peter is safe beside the twins on the carpet, he puts his hand out for the light. "Come on, I'll cover you now."

Alice's lips press tight together. She can't stop thinking about what her mother said. That if they let the boy out, the monsters will be free too. "Sensitive and brave," she whispers to herself. "Brave and sensitive."

In the cave Khalil feels like a leaf in the wind. His heart is broken by the biggest monster. He wants to go home, but knows he can't go back. He wants the familiar, but knows the monsters destroyed it in their blind rage. He wants his mother.

The biggest monster surges forward, but Khalil scoots closer to the trap door.

"Come on," Alice urges. "Please come out of there."

He hurts inside so bad; his new friends don't fill the gap of loss.

Then Jane says, "The other children from your village are going to need help. You have to be brave and come out first. Letting the monsters eat you won't help anyone."

A mix of emotions makes Khalil shake so hard he is afraid he will slip from the damp rocks. "I can't," he whispers.

"You won't be alone," Peter promises.

The biggest monster hisses and moves closer to Khalil, but the boy stops shaking. "You were once my mother, Amena," he says to the monster. "We rowed across the ocean together. If there is anything inside of you that remembers me, please let me by."

The monster opens and shuts its mouth, the teeth sliding past each other with a sickening sound. It appears confused and scratches at the sewn shut eyes with dirty claws. Khalil feels a moment of illicit hope, that his mother is inside and can be saved. The claws rake down the monster's cheeks and a smell seeps out so rotten that

121

Khalil gags. No, there is nothing left of his mother in there except some tickle of memory responding to his voice or maybe his scent. She keeps scratching at her body and Khalil understands that this confusion is all there is.

"Thank you for protecting me," he gasps. "Thank you for—" He doesn't know what to say because crying 'I love you' to this rotten salamander creature doesn't feel right, but ignoring her doesn't either. "Thank you," he finishes.

Khalil turns away and scrambles through the hole. After he's through, the children slam the trap door down and hear scratching from underneath.

Peter puts an arm around Khalil's slumped shoulders. "Come with me, my friend."

❧

When Mother has called the children for dinner, Khalil walks into the kitchen wearing Peter's clothes: athletic shorts, t-shirt, and Steelers socks. They are large on him and he has to hitch up the shorts.

Alice pats the chair next to her. "You sit here."

Mother glances at the boy from the basement and then speaks to the wall that is Father's newspaper. "I found some new light switch covers for the bedrooms. I think they'll add a touch of class."

Jane clears her throat until Mother looks at her. "Mother," says Jane. "You forgot to set the place for Peter again."

They all know that this is the moment when Mother can speak up, say that Peter left for school, but Jane is willing to gamble. Mother has ignored the fact that there are children who are lost, crying in the darkness across the ocean, and need a place to stay. She wants to think about her house and her work and her normal routine. But it is another thing, Jane knows, to look at the actual child in the actual kitchen and make the choice to ignore him.

Khalil holds his breath. Everything is so strange and different. He is a refugee; his family is dead and he has nowhere else to go. He feels a hand reaching for his under the table and gives Alice a grateful look. He appreciates the plan that Peter, Jane, and Alice made: that he would be Peter while the real Peter was at school, but Khalil does not want to be Peter. He is not ashamed of his village or his mother and he will not dishonor her sacrifice. He pushes himself to a standing position and announces: "My name is Khalil. I am from Omran and I need a place to live until I can save the other families from my village."

Father's newspaper sinks until his eyes peep over the top edge.

Mother throws a wild look around the kitchen as if afraid that the house will tumble down. Maybe it will. She closes her eyes and steadies herself against the table. "We should leave. Walk away right now."

Alice notices that Mother's closed eyelashes resemble stitches, crisscrossing her cheeks. She thinks that maybe the sightless ghuls were not confined to Omran in the first place. That maybe there are monsters inside of everyone.

After two beats of Jane's heart, Mother's eyes open and the illusion of stitches disappears. Jane knows she has won. Kindly, she says, "We have to stay. We have to do the next right thing. And then the next. That's all we can do."

Mother turns away from the table and brings back a plate, silverware, and napkin.

Dad says grace and snaps up his newspaper again.

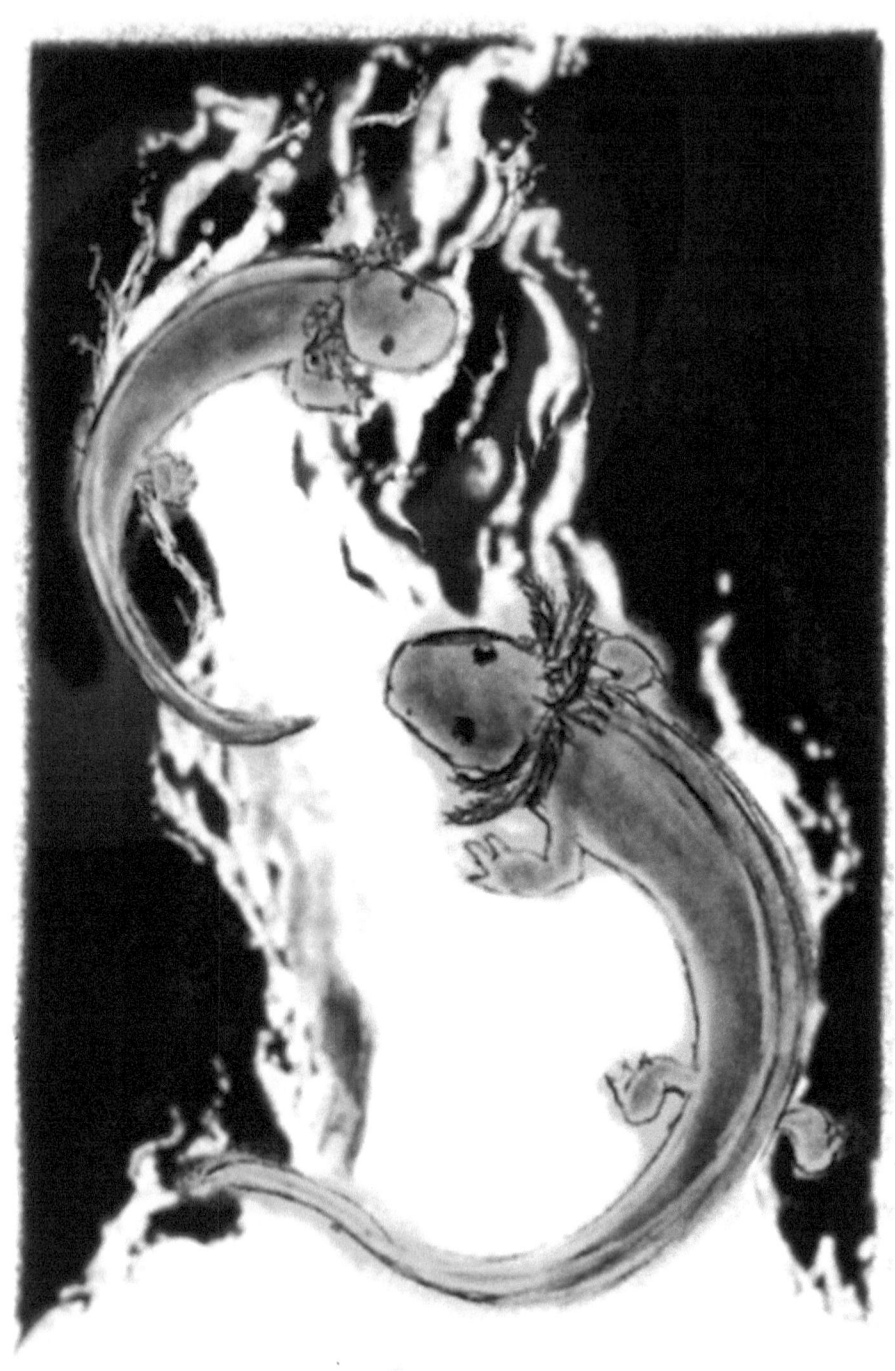

MAMA SALAMANDER

With a crackle, brilliant orange and red surrounded mother and daughter.
The flames grew higher and hotter. They stretched beyond the stone fireplace.

Mama Salamander

The bright yellow stars had dulled on Scora's back when she came home from school, her movements empty of joy. Mama's eyes narrowed from her spot on the wall. Her tail flicked like a metronome. Nearby, water dripped down from the roof of the cottage to the soft moss that grew on the floor. Scora did not look up. She crept to her side of the cottage and took out her basket of smooth stones, lining them up by order of preference.

Mama Salamander stalked the stone walls of the cottage, up and down having no meaning, as she watched the winter twilight deepen. And when darkness came, mother and daughter left to hunt. Their bodies matched: smooth moist skin, three toes on each front foot, four toes on the back, beautiful black coloring with yellow stars. *Salamandra Salamandra*. Fire salamanders.

"They made fun of me today," Scora said.

Mama lunged forward, her sticky tongue shot out and grabbed a centipede. It wriggled. Mama's tongue retracted. The centipede disappeared in a gulp.

"Whatever for?" Mama asked. It had never occurred to her that anyone might find a single imperfection in her Scora.

"At lunchtime. They said my spider was gross. I had to throw it away." Scora's triangular head sank to the ground as if it were too heavy. "They said I was gross for eating it."

"They would be so lucky to have spiders for lunch. I shall come and burn them all up." Mama crept forward through the forest, approaching the river. The air smelled fertile, the dirt felt soft. Quick digging motions and Mama exposed a writhing earthworm for Scora.

Scora's tongue flicked out. She ate.

Mama nodded with satisfaction. The earthworm would bring back the shine in Scora's yellow stars.

"You can't burn them all up," Scora said. "I'll get in trouble."

They slithered home.

"They said they wouldn't be my friend because I had no hair to comb."

"Your body is sleek and elegant. I shall burn off their hair and then they will have neither hair nor messy fur."

"No, Mama. Then everyone at school will be scared of me."

Mama crawled into the large stone fireplace that made up the entire back wall of the cottage. "Come to me, daughter. Let me hold you."

Scora sank against her mother, pressing cheek to chest. "Dawnel said that I have to give her my smooth stones tomorrow or she will tell everyone in the class to not be my friend."

"You spent a lot of time searching the riverbank for those stones," Mama said. "Do you want to give them away?"

Scora shook her head. "But I want to have friends. Everyone likes Dawnel. They'll listen to everything she says."

"She sounds like a picky, hairy child to me."

Scora sighed.

"We are elementals," Mama said. "Our fire comes from our hearts." Mama turned her attention inwards, gathering her heart force. With a whoosh of air, heat spread from belly through permeable skin. Mama burst into flames.

"You're beautiful, Mama."

"And you are brave, little Scora. Words cannot hurt you any more than my flames can. Go to school tomorrow and hold your head high. Speak up for yourself."

Back and forth Scora waved her paw through the flame. "I don't know how to talk to Dawnel."

Mama's eyes closed halfway in enjoyment of the fire. Hungry flames licked at the stones of the fireplace. "Put your foot over your heart and with each breath imagine the heat building around your heart and through your belly."

Scora's three toes rested against her skin. Eyes closed, little flames teased at her head and at her tail.

"More," crooned Mama. "More with each exhale. Embrace the fire."

With a crackle, brilliant orange and red surrounded mother and daughter. The flames grew higher and hotter. They stretched beyond the stone fireplace. Scora's wicker basket, left on the floor beside the line of river stones, caught on fire.

"No," Scora cried out. The flames shrank to an inch above her skin.

Mama slapped the burning basket with her tail until the wicker fell apart in a shower of sparks, dying on the stone floor, scattering among the stones.

"I didn't mean to burn it up," said Scora.

"Nonetheless, it cannot be put back together," Mama said. She examined her tail. "Remember this when you talk to Dawnel tomorrow. Anger feels good. It burns fast and hard, but the flames cannot be controlled."

"I want to speak the warmth of the fire, but not the burn." More confident, Scora nodded. "Be brave without being mean. I know what to say."

⚜

When it was time for school again, Mama Salamander went too. She flicked her tail while the children filed inside. Scora gave her a little wave before disappearing. Mama turned to the other mothers. Mama Mermaid leaning on the edge of her portable aquarium, playing with her blue hair while she chatted with the manticore and the harpy. The phoenix—sister fire elemental—preened her feathers.

"So," Mama said. She turned her attention inward and gathered her heart force. Her triangular mouth smiled to reveal nubbins of teeth. "Which of you is Dawnel's mother?"

Finders Keepers

The Finding Stone warmed Rachel Deneuve's hand, a sensation confirming that she was closing in on the goal at the end of the wooden pathway. Get to the goal, hand over the message, and then she could go home. Except, of course, it was never that easy when Supernaturals were concerned. Each god or goddess had their own set of rules for each territory, some actively torturing humans and others enjoying the thrill of playing with mortals. As if that wasn't bad enough, Captain Lewis had been sent as her bodyguard. Quite ironic when he was the reason she'd been sent on this mission in the first place. Rachel pushed damp auburn hair away from her neck. The air was both hot and stuffy despite their being in a shaded canyon.

Indeed, the pathway might have been an invitation for a nice meander through the forest, but Rachel knew better. Green lichen covered the steep mountainsides making a 'V'-shape with the pathway at the bottom. This made it easy to be attacked from above but hard to escape. High above, trees filtered the light. Rachel couldn't identify their species. Maybe something native to Wisconsin or maybe something that grew after the sky broke open and ancient Mesopotamian gods fell to Earth in the form of destructive firestorms. Cities burned and now reality rebuilt itself in the strange image of myths that humans barely remembered. Normal had become a magic-based dystopia imposed on humans by the whims of capricious Supernaturals. For Rachel, survival meant walking the blade of serving one of the new deities, the dragon-goddess Nammu.

Ahead, maybe another quarter of a mile, wooden stairs descended to a glade. A tall metal arch spanned the stairs with circular mirrors embedded in the arabesques.

"I can see the fifth gate." Wind pulled at the edges of her coat and ruffled the ferns growing from crevices in the rocks. "Are you going to stay here?"

"Never thought I'd be happy to see the fifth gate of Hell," Captain Lewis said, emerging around a curve of the path, bow and quiver across his back. He was tall with broad shoulders—as an artist Rachel could admire his proportions even if she found him personally overbearing. The sides of his head were shaved, leaving a sleek blond ponytail on top. His eyes were a curious shade of seaglass blue and a pale shadow ringed his eye—a scar from an encounter with the corrupt energy of a two-headed moose soon after the Supernaturals had taken over. At his side, Caesar, a black wolf the size of a pony, blinked yellow eyes.

"Kur," Rachel corrected, turning in one direction and then the other. "The Sumerians call the Underworld 'Kur'."

Wind in the trees above created an eerie moaning sound as the bare branches rubbed against each other. The air seemed to shiver and Rachel felt a familiar tingling sensation.

"There's an *etemmu* storm coming." Dread settled in Rachel's stomach. When the gods broke free from their celestial prison, they had to break the lock—the body of Shamash, god of justice. As Shamash's body unraveled, his *etemmu* or lifeforce, rained down. Now the power gathered in toxic pockets and created sudden storms of power that swept the land with chaotic abandon, creating mutations in plants and animals and causing geographic changes before dispersing.

"This canyon will funnel the storm," Lewis said. "I don't want to see what hellscape that will cause."

Rachel bit back a sarcastic *No kidding* and settled for, "Right." Short answers so that they wouldn't get into a fight.

The storm hit with a flash of blue lightning and a gust of wind. To Rachel, who'd learned how to manipulate *etemmu*, it looked like the air was filled with gold glitter. Then came an itching sensation under her skin and black dots swam across her vision as if she would faint. Rachel stumbled, grabbing onto the railing of the pathway.

Behind her, Lewis yelled, "Run for the gate."

The gate was stable. She could see the *etemmu* pelting the opening and being repulsed, but the rest of the world heaved and groaned.

A chunk of rock fell down by her feet, the fern on top vibrating like the feather of a cap.

Another groaning sound as the mountain on her right shifted, the lumber of the walkway buckling as the support underneath gave way.

"Come on." Lewis grabbed her arm. "You're the one who has to deliver the message, not me."

Caesar ran ahead, his body a dark shadow as he picked a path through the wreckage of the pathway.

In a shower of pebbles and dust, the mountain cracked open. Long humanoid fingers tipped with sharp fingernails emerged from the crack, scraping the opening wider. A roar came from inside and then chunks of rock fell away as a beast-woman emerged.

Lamashtu is awake. The words rippled through Rachel and she didn't know if she heard them or if they came from some ancient part of her human mind.

Lamashtu was a hybrid of nightmares with a lioness' head topped by a donkey's ears, a hairy humanoid body about seven feet tall, and the feet of a raptor. She crouched on the mountainside with her nose to the sky as the storm dissipated.

"Yeah, I'm hating Hell right about now." In a smooth motion Lewis nocked his bow and pointed it at the creature.

Rachel's heart pounded like she'd binged espressos, but she walked forward along the pathway. Lamashtu was obviously a predator. Running would attract attention and spark the prey drive.

Near the gate Caesar stood at attention on top of a boulder, watching.

She could hear Lewis walking behind. And then there was a gap in the broken walkway. There should have been forest floor a few feet below, but with the mountain's shifting there was a steep drop into darkness.

"Take off your backpack." Without waiting, Lewis tugged on it. "You'll jump across and then I'll throw our packs over and come after."

"Maybe—" She needed to think this through.

From her spot on the mountainside, Lamashtu exposed her teeth and made a series of guttural sounds that sounded like ragged panting. The sound echoed off the canyon walls and settled in Rachel's bones.

"Collegiate lacrosse player, current captain of New Babylon's military. Your goddess-assigned bodyguard." He set her pack down. "I'm sure."

Rachel eyed the gap again. Once upon a time, before the Mesopotamian gods returned, she'd been an art historian and hobby artist and then a stay-at-home mom. Adam. That single image of her teenaged son steadied Rachel. She backed up on the pathway and then she ran forward, pumping her arms for momentum.

Rachel pushed off at the edge of the walkway and seemed to hover over the darkness below before landing on the other side. Adrenaline coursed through her and Rachel turned back to grin at Lewis.

Her pride turned to horror. "Behind you," she screamed, but Lewis already had the bow up.

Lamashtu's claws dug into the rocks as she leaped down the mountain in a zigzag pattern with inelegant strength, her donkey ears flapping behind. Lewis's first arrow missed, but the second lodged in her shoulder. The creature screamed and bared her canines, spit stretching across her open maw.

A third arrow thudded into Lamashtu's stomach and she leaped at Lewis, falling on top of him with her fingers and talons extended.

Rachel felt the pathway vibrating a second before Caesar charged past her, leaping the gap and hitting the beast-woman in mid-flight so that she landed on her side and rolled to her back with the wolf at her throat.

Lewis had ducked out of the way and now he ran forward with a knife.

Lamashtu bucked her hips and pushed Caesar away from her with long arms. Then she dug her pointed fingernails into the wolf's sides like skewers before lifting him up and throwing him against the mountain.

Caesar hit hard and then slid down into the ferns, eyes closed.

Lewis closed with Lamashtu, but with feline power she jumped to her feet and into a crouch.

They circled and then Lewis lunged forward, his knife slicing along her ribs. He'd miscalculated her reach, though, and she grabbed him into a bear hug. He was too close to be effective with the blade.

Lamashtu looked down into his face and roared, spittle flying out, but then her nose quivered. She whipped her head to stare at Rachel's hand.

Rachel looked at the Finding Stone. Lamashtu must sense the *etemmu*. Rachel sprinted towards the Fifth Gate of Kur.

A heavy thud shook the walkway behind Rachel and then bird talons scraped against the wood. Rachel was steps away from the gate when fingernails clawed her back, a burning sensation from her neck down to her hip. Rachel whipped around, a knife in her right hand and the Finding Stone in her left.

"Want this?"

The creature's putrid breath washed over Rachel as Lamashtu roared.

Rachel heaved the Finding Stone back toward the break in the pathway. Lamashtu scrambled for it like a cat chasing a ball, right into where Lewis and Caesar, a retaliatory glint in his eyes, waited.

A final arrow plunged into Lamashtu's eye and Caesar jumped on the back of the beast-woman, worrying at her neck and dragging her to the gap. One final shake of the wolf's head and Lamashtu's body plunged down, disappearing. A full minute later there was a splash of water.

Rachel walked forward and picked up the Finding Stone.

"Gods damn." Lewis touched the top of Caesar's head and the wolf whined. "You're a tough old man."

The three of them limped through the fifth gate. In the distance, a white bridge stretched across a river and ended abruptly less than halfway to the other side.

"We'll have to camp tonight and start fresh." Lewis set down the two packs he'd been carrying.

"No, we need to keep going." Rachel watched as the sun sank toward the horizon, pink and orange hues an elegant background for the bridge and the rippling water. "We're running out of time to find Ereshkigal."

"I know why you're in a hurry, but wandering around in the dark won't get you back to your son." Lewis unpacked the bedroll and smoothed a spot for a fire. "And Caesar needs to rest. That Lamashtu-thing hurt him."

She wanted to stamp her feet, but this wasn't his fault. Rachel's shoulders slumped. "Alright."

She whistled for Caesar and made a sound of sympathy as the black wolf limped over.

Rachel rubbed at her wrist where the metal disc embedded in her skin was a symbol of the deal she'd made: to save her son Adam she'd become indebted to the goddess Nammu. That's why she had to deliver the Finding Stone to Ereshkigal before she was allowed to go home to her son.

Closing her eyes, Rachel sank into a meditative state until her hands began to tingle. Then she reached for the wolf and threaded her hands into his fur. He whined and leaned into her as her energy connected with his. She moved their *etemmu* through his body, finding injuries to stop the internal bleeding and tamping down inflammation. He'd still be sore and need to rest, and he'd definitely have scars from Lamashtu's nails, but his life wasn't in danger anymore.

When Rachel came out of the healing trance, Lewis had finished setting up camp to the side of the gate and built a small fire against the evening's chill. He handed her a bowl of soup heated over the fire. Thank goodness that some pre-packaged food was still available.

After dinner they settled on logs close enough that the fire's warmth could reach their outstretched hands. Darkness encroached, obscuring details around the camp.

"You hum when you heal."

"What?" Lost in her thoughts, Rachel looked up from where she snuggled into her blanket.

"I said—"

"No, I—"

They stared at the fire as it popped and crackled. She hadn't chosen the mission and he hadn't chosen to accompany her. They were pawns of whatever game the gods played as they set up territories like the boardgame Risk. "I'll be happy to get back to my home and my bed and my son." Adam. Thirteen years old. Hazel eyes, a propensity to wear athletic shorts and t-shirts no matter the weather, and an ability to eat his own weight in food when the mood struck.

Lewis snorted. "You talk about home a lot."

"Family is everything." She adjusted the blanket. "And when you're separated, all you have are memories. They hold truth, meaning, the why for everything we do. What could be worth more?" She leaned forward to feed a stick to the fire. Pine sap bubbled from the branch and the smell perfumed the air. "I'm sure the consularis is worried about you." The consularis of New Babylon was Captain Lewis's soon to be father-in-law.

"He's worried about missing the captain of his guard, not about me personally."

"Well, Vishni misses you-you." Rachel gestured at him. "And congratulations on the baby."

He threw a stick into the fire. Caesar whined. Rachel had learned that the wolf was Lewis's emotional barometer, but she wasn't sure why he'd be angry or hurt that she was wishing his family well.

"You're going back to your home when we're done." He wasn't looking at her.

"Yes." Rachel and Adam lived in An's territory. By god standards he was both reasonable and tolerant. By anyone else's standards he was cranky and chaotic like the lightning he threw around.

"And not going back to New Babylon."

Rachel stared into the fire. He was asking if she could keep a secret. "Goddess willing, I never want to see New Babylon again."

He nodded as if agreeing with himself, took a breath, and said, "It's not mine."

It took Rachel a moment. "You travel a lot…the timing. It could."

"No, it couldn't. Vishni and I never slept together." He waved his hand in the air as if reaching for words. "Her father's conservative. He's priest of the city. I wanted to wait till after the ceremony."

He must be so hurt. And his pride. All of New Babylon looking on.

Some kind of night bird called out and was answered from a different direction. Caesar's ears pricked up and then he laid his head on his paws again.

"I hate her."

Lewis was a soldier—stoic and expected to be. There wouldn't be a single person in New Babylon that he could tell. He'd be charged with treason and either banished or executed.

Between the darkness and Rachel's silence, he seemed to lose his ability to hold his thoughts inside.

"Just like my mother." He grabbed a large branch from the forest and thrust it into the fire, sparks shooting up into shapes that hinted at meaning, but flickered out before Rachel could read them. "You're always talking about your son and your home, but that's not my experience. My mom was just like Vishni. My dad was a good man, a military man, and she cheated on him and then left us. Those are my memories."

Caesar surged to his feet, black against the forest's darkness. His tail twitched as he watched Rachal.

"Are they a boy's memories or a man's memories?"

"What do you mean?"

Rachel thought about her life with Adam's father, the anger and loss she'd felt when finally understanding that neither of them had been perfect; both had been guilty of harsh words and unkindness. "Each time you revisit a memory it's different than when it happened because you are different. You bring more maturity, experience, and understanding to that memory and maybe you start to see something that you missed."

"I don't care to revisit those memories. I don't want to see something that I missed. I know what happened and that's enough."

Caesar pointed his nose at the sky and howled, a mournful sound that made Rachel want to cover her ears.

"That's why Caesar is my best friend. He's the only one I trust." They melted into the night. "We'll patrol the perimeter."

Rachel poked at the fire. She wanted to go home and hold Adam. Breathe in his teenager boy stink and kiss him as he ducked away. She wanted to assure him she hadn't left him behind on purpose. She wondered if he was thinking about her at this moment, what memories he was revisiting.

❧

In the morning Rachel led the way to the bridge, Finding Stone held in front of her. The bridge was a startling pure white with a gritty texture. Limestone, she guessed. Elaborate arches reached

136

down into green water. The river stretched about two hundred feet across, but the bridge, four arches in, ended in a jagged line.

"That's stupid," Captain Lewis said, his tone flat. "It doesn't go anywhere."

Rachel ground her teeth. Apparently last night's openness had been replaced by surliness.

There was a tug like a fish pulling on a line. Extending her arm, Rachel walked forward. Footsteps behind told her that the man and wolf followed. The stone became hot between the third and fourth arch and then cooled as Rachel continued to the jagged edge of the bridge. She turned and walked back to the space where the Finding Stone was hot and raked the air with her other hand.

"What are you doing?"

"Trying to find the entrance."

"You look ridiculous." Captain Lewis shook his head. "Is the problem with the magic or with you?"

"You could help me."

"How," he said, throwing his hands in the air. "We're on an empty, broken bridge. You said gods and goddesses like to be up high, close to the heavens. I didn't know they could have invisible temples too…"

Rachel frowned. "They do like to be up high," her fingers drummed against the Finding Stone, "unless, perhaps, you are the goddess of the underworld."

Rachel went to the side of the bridge and held her fist over, toward the green water flowing over in fast eddies. The Finding Stone burned in her hand and Rachel yanked her hand back, expecting to see blisters. She set the rock aside. "I'm going in."

"You can't." Captain Lewis leaned over the side. "Look at how that water plant's branches are being pulled by the current. Besides, you have no idea what's down there."

Rachel shivered. He was right. Nothing could be seen through the opaque water and the only thing on top was some type of plant with leaves so green they were almost black. The leaves seemed somehow ominous, as if they were teeth in a watery mouth. She felt sick. And certain. "That's it." She pointed to the mouth. "The sixth entrance." She removed her coat, pack, and boots before climbing down the side of the bridge to the arch's platform a couple feet above the water.

Wind whipped at her hair. The water seemed to respond to her distress, the top choppy as it smacked into the side of the bridge with a rough sound. The leaves, rubbing against each other, released a strange dark scent. Her heart stuttered against her ribs in frantic communication that it did not approve of her intentions. Rachel spoke to her heart silently, seizing those images of Adam that she'd pushed away before. Her son as a newborn with perfect little fingers and toes, crying with a skinned knee, night time fears that only she could kiss away. Then, her memory flashed to the minutes before she'd left New Babylon. His almost-man's eyes as he'd given her a hug and told her to drink water because she always complained about being thirsty, but never drank. Roles reversed and her pride and wonder at how he'd grown. It was unthinkable that she'd never see Adam again.

She jumped.

Her arms flapped as if she could fly. Cold water shocked her, the liquid more viscous than expected. Rachel opened her eyes. They stung, but she forced them to remain open. All was coated green, but the surface, a golden curtain of *etemmu* above, beckoned her to leave. The tangle of leaves seen from above now resolved into the topmost branches of a giant white tree. The trunk descended farther than Rachel's eyes could see. Rachel's lungs screamed for oxygen and she exhaled. The bubbles floated like lazy balloons, spreading in all directions. This wasn't natural; she had entered sacred space. Panic erupted into a burning sensation along Rachel's veins from heart to fingertips. Light flickered in the corner of her eyes. Her limbs grew heavy.

I am dying.

She kicked for the surface, but the liquid gel resisted. The light appeared again, moving across her vision. Shapes resolved into pillars and a throne. And then hands pulled her up.

Rachel collapsed, shaking, her stomach cramping. She gagged again and again. Someone rubbed her arms and legs. She wanted to tell them to stop, that it hurt, and then Rachel realized it was Captain Lewis, beside her on one of the limestone arches.

"You're wet," she said, noticing his clothing. "You went in too."

"That's my job, remember? Caesar and I are supposed to guard the messenger." His voice was grim, mouth set in a straight line. "You stayed under a long time. Are you satisfied that she's not down there?"

"Unfortunately," Rachel said, voice hoarse, "Now I know that she is."

Captain Lewis shook his head, but Rachel knew the throne room was no death vision. "I saw the entrance when I was drowning." Rachel rubbed her face. Her eyes felt tired and somehow sticky from the green water, her chest burned. "Makes sense, right? You have to be dying or dead to speak to a goddess of the underworld."

From the bridge overhead, Caesar whined and his claws scraped against the side.

"If we know she's down there," Captain Lewis said, "can't you just drop the message in the water and be done with it?"

Rachel gave a weak laugh. "I think this requires a hand delivery."

Captain Lewis frowned. "And if you die?"

Rachel was surprised to hear genuine curiosity in his voice, as if he thought her opinion mattered.

"No big deal," she said, wringing out her water-darkened hair. "That's why Nammu chose us. If we die, she'll choose more humans and send them until the message gets through."

He whistled. "Nothing like realizing you're a pawn."

"We're always pawns when the gods play." Rachel pressed her lips together.

"Fine." Captain Lewis rubbed his hands together. "How do we get Ereshkigal's attention?"

"I surfaced just as I saw the temple. I needed another couple seconds."

"So, you're going in again?" He shook his head. "You're exhausted."

"Only my face has to be in." Rachel swallowed. "But you're going to have to hold me down."

He jerked back. "You want me to kill you?"

"I want you to pull me up at the last possible second. We'll work out a signal." Rachel cleared her throat. "That was the deal. We have to deliver the message if we want to see our…home." She'd been going to say "family" and stopped herself, not wanting to bring up Vishni.

She saw him thinking, flipping through alternatives. She saw when his eyes went hard and she couldn't help feeling offended that it took only seconds for him to agree. Rachel lowered to her belly and put her head over the viscous green liquid.

"If something happens, please send a message to Adam." She stared at the tree leaves in the water. "Don't let him think that I abandoned him."

"He would never think that," Captain Lewis said with an edge to his voice. "You're a good mother. Not like," he cleared his throat as if swallowing words. "I'll get you back to your son."

"Captain—"

"Just accept my compliment. I said you were a good mother. That's all you get."

Rachel closed her eyes to focus before the final plunge. Goddesses needed humans to fear them or love them—human emotion and *etemmu* made them stronger. What could she offer to get Ereshkigal's attention? It would, of course, have to be a sacrifice. She thought of the bubbles floating like balloons when she'd been underwater before. She thought of Adam, her son. And then she nodded that she was ready.

Captain Lewis's hand was firm on the back of her head as he pushed down. Her face splashed into the leaves. Letting the memory of Adam's face fill her mind—his hazel eyes and brown hair that smelled of sunshine and sweat—Rachel exhaled a bubble, directing her *etemmu*, same as she used when accessing the Finding Stone. Slowly an image appeared inside the bubble. Adam with his first missing tooth, proudly holding it up before putting it under his pillow for the tooth fairy.

The memory floated away and Rachel felt a sting of loss. Determined, she conjured another memory. Adam as a toddler, sleeping on his belly with his diapered rump in the air, passed out when he was trying to give up his morning nap. She blew the bubble and watched it float down.

She was running out of air, but there was no light from below, no sign of the goddess. Rachel shifted her shoulders against Captain Lewis's pressure, but he didn't move. She'd done the best she could, he had to let her up. Rachel tried to pull her head up, every instinct in her body screaming for air. She waved her left hand in the air in the prearranged signal. Strong hands held her in place. She thrashed her body, but Captain Lewis was too strong.

Rachel opened her mouth to scream and little bubbles rushed out, her memories bleeding into them uncontrolled, not the ones she'd chosen. Her gaze darkened as she inhaled water, desperate.

Captain Lewis yanked her up, liquid sluicing off her hair and face. Her mouth was still open in a scream. He turned her to the side and she heaved again and again, her tongue filling her mouth, fingers trying to grab water out of her throat, tears streaming down her face.

When she was able to calm down, he started talking, but she couldn't hear. He gave her a little shake and Rachel looked at him through blurred vision.

"I couldn't bring you up. Something was fighting with me." He closed her eyelids with the pads of his fingers. "You've broken blood vessels in your eyes. Otherwise, are you okay?"

"No," she whimpered. "I've lost something. So many somethings, but I don't know how or why."

"We're leaving." His arms were underneath her, about to pick her up.

A rustling sound filled Rachel's mind. She opened her broken eyes to see the water parting at the top of the submerged tree.

From the bridge, the large black wolf stared at the water and growled a warning.

The goddess ascended through the water until she hovered above the surface. She looked youthful with flawless dark skin and wearing a simple white dress. Tiny braids coiled into a mass on top of her head. Her eyes were large with kohl drawing up at the ends. Wings peeked over her shoulders and stretched down her back. In her hands she held what looked like soap bubbles.

"You've drawn my attention with your gifts." Her voice was velvet. Rachel didn't want her to stop talking. It looked, from Captain Lewis's struck expression, that he felt the same. Distracted, he pulled his arms from underneath Rachel and stood up.

"You may enter Ganzir, my palace." Ereshkigal pressed her extended fingertips together and then spread them apart until a large bubble formed. Then she blew the bubble until it encompassed Lewis and Rachel.

Mesmerized, Rachel touched the sides. It felt gelatinous.

"Can you not pop it, please?" Lewis said.

Before she could retort, the bubble moved over the water.

Up on the bridge, Caesar stalked back and forth, his yellow eyes full of anxiety.

"We'll be back," Rachel promised, having no idea if it was true. How many mortals were allowed to leave Kur once they'd entered?

The bubble descended through the darkness, the goddess Ereshkigal floating before them, her dress drifting in the current. Golden *etemmu* sparkled in the water like fairy lights. Then Ganzir materialized beneath them.

A palace made of white marble sat on top of boat wreckages and piles of gold coins and sparkling jewels enclosed by a coral reef. At the base of the steps a full diving suit stood at attention. A green and blue sea serpent coiled through the coins, looking up at them and then diving back in. The trunk of the tree descended past the wreckages into the unknown.

The bubble floated into the temple through pillars with octopi wrapped around in living decoration. One squirted ink as they went past. Crabs skuttled sideways on the steps.

"The seventh gate," Rachel whispered.

Once inside Ganzir, the bubbles popped. Rachel and Lewis dropped to the floor. There was no water inside the palace; instead, a bubble must be keeping it out. Ereshkigal had taken a seat on a throne with the back in the shape of an open shell. Next to her stood an older man with white hair wearing a butler's uniform, including white gloves.

Rachel placed a hand at her hip and hinged into a bow. She'd learned about the vanities of the gods through her interactions with Nammu. For example, there was no such thing as too much flattery. "Thank you, gracious Ereshkigal, for receiving us. Your palace is stunning. I especially admire the Corinthian columns and the way your throne incorporates Botticelli's idea of beauty in a goddess."

"Too bad he was unaware of what was myth and what was real." Ereskigal raised her eyebrows. "But I do love decorating from the various time periods. It creates an eclectic yet timeless aesthetic."

"Indeed," Rachel murmured. "You are the epitome of taste."

Ereshkigal extended a hand. "You present yourself well and are welcome in Ganzir."

They all turned to Lewis.

"Uh." He mimicked Rachel's bow. "I like your man in the uniform and the way the octopus wrap their legs around the columns."

Rachel pressed her lips together and hoped they weren't about to be fed to the sea serpent outside.

"Also, they would make very good weapons because they have eight legs."

The only sound was the jangle of coins as the sea serpent adjusted.

Then Ereshkigal laughed and her attendant ventured a tiny giggle and rocked back and forth in his shiny shoes.

"You have confidence, mortal. You, too, are welcome." She gestured to her attendant. "This is my dear Neti. He's been with me for countless years."

"Truly countless," Neti simpered.

Suddenly Lamashtu appeared from the hallway behind the throne. Her body showed the bloody marks that Lewis and Caesar had inflicted. With a snarl she arced toward Rachel.

Rachel ducked as Lewis grabbed his bow and nocked an arrow.

"How dare you attack those for whom I have offered welcome."

Ereshkigal did not raise her voice, but Lamashtu's body froze in midair, her snarl locked on her lioness face and the donkey ears jutting back.

Standing up and walking down to Lamashtu, Ereshkigal was like a ballerina, like music. Rachel's mind struggled to come up with a comparison that revealed the power and grace of the goddess.

Ereshkigal touched Lamashtu and bubbles floated out of the creature's mouth—bubbles that contained images of Rachel, Lewis, and Caesar.

"As punishment, I have taken her memories of you. She will not remember her vendetta."

"Thank you," Lewis said.

"Although she will keep her feelings and will not like you, she won't know why."

"Um." Lewis looked to Rachel and raised his eyebrows.

She shrugged. What did he want her to say?

"Return Lamashtu to storage. When she's healed, I'll place her outside the second gate as a deterrent to visitors." Ereshkigal returned to the throne as Neti hurried forward and grabbed Lamashtu's foot, pulling her through air like she was a balloon. "Now, tell me why you two have come."

"Nammu sends her regards and a personal message." Rachel offered the Finding Stone with trembling hands.

Ereshkigal took the stone and its center glowed as she stared at it. When the glow had faded, she handed the stone to Neti with a curt nod.

"That's it, right?" Lewis asked Rachel. "Now you can go home to Adam."

Rachel frowned. "Who?"

"Bad joke." He fidgeted. "Your son. Your entire reason for everything you do? The one that I had to hear about this entire trip every time you got homesick for him?"

Rachel stared at Lewis. Her hands started shaking and she didn't understand what he was saying or why. She didn't know anyone named Adam, but there was a hole inside of her.

"What do you remember about Adam? About your home?"

Rachel shook her head. The questions echoed inside her mind. She didn't know who she was or what she wanted. She looked to Lewis, "Please," she said. She felt helpless, not even knowing what had been taken from her. "Help me."

Lewis's expression turned cold and hard as he pivoted to face the goddess on the throne.

"Hey," Captain Lewis made a growling sound that could have come from Caesar's throat. He stepped toward the throne. "What did you do to Rachel? The same thing you did to the lion-donkey?"

Returning to the room, Neti immediately placed himself in front of the throne.

Rachel, unsure what he was talking about, watched the goddess for a clue to understand this conversation. She couldn't stop shaking.

"She offered me memories. I accepted them." Ereshkigal held up her cupped hands and bubbles floated into the air around her. Bubbles full of a blond-haired baby and a brown-haired young man that was surely the same child. Rachel's heart pinged with loss, but nothing else happened.

"There's no way she offered those," Lewis said. "You took them."

"You will not speak to a goddess that way, mortal," Neti said. He pulled at his white gloves.

"Finders keepers." Ereshkigal tilted her head. "Why shouldn't I keep them?"

"Because they mean everything to her. It's who she is and the story that helps her navigate the world and what she uses to make choices. It's not fair."

"Fair? The world is not fair, human. Is it fair that I was assigned to rule the underworld while the rest of my family walks among the living?" Ereshkigal shook her head until the braids on her head vibrated. "Is it fair that I have no experiences of my own because I am confined to my watery kingdom?"

"At least give her one back so that she knows she has a son."

"What will you give me in return?"

"You keep the memories because you can't make your own." Captain Lewis paced for a moment before pointing at Geshtinanna. "You made a deal with her, right? That she and her brother could exchange places." He swallowed. "Fine. I'll give you a memory of mine."

Ereshkigal extended her tongue and licked one of the bubbles. Her eyes dropped to half-mast and she gave a sensuous shudder. "Make it good and I'll consider."

"Full of all the emotion you could want." He gave a bitter laugh.

Rachel sank to the floor. Her insides had grown cold. There was no reason to stand. No reason to do anything.

Captain Lewis nodded his head once.

Ereshkigal blew a bubble toward Rachel so that it hovered right at her temple. There was a young teenager inside with a serious expression.

Rachel reached out a shaking finger.

Pop.

The memory of Adam rushed in, the smell of his hair, feel of his arms around her, the concern in his eyes as he comforted her in the final minutes before she had to leave New Babylon. "I'll meet you at home," he'd said. "Stay safe and hurry back. I love you."

The bubble pieced itself together and floated toward Captain Lewis. He reached out to touch it and then looked at Rachel. He opened his mouth as if to ask something, but no words came out.

"I remember him," Rachel whispered.

"Have you changed your mind?" Erishkigal asked. Her fingers drummed against the throne's arm. "Don't tease me, human."

"I haven't changed my mind." He thrust his hand towards the bubble and then shuddered as a woman with the same blue eyes as

Captain Lewis appeared inside the bubble. He clenched his teeth and looked away.

Rachel hated the goddess for her casual cruelty. Whatever the memory was, it pained Lewis both to remember it and to lose it.

The memory bubble floated back to the goddess.

Ereshkigal inspected the memory. Her wings fluttered. "This one is delicious. Layers of pain and love and betrayal. I'll save that one." The goddess stepped down from the throne and disappeared into the hallway beyond. Neti trotted after her. Geshtinanna ignored them as she continued writing in the giant book.

Water began to seep into Ganzir, flowing over the steps and into the throne room. It lapped against the Corinthian columns. The octopi began to slide down.

"We should ask her for a bubble to get to the surface," Rachel said. She still felt faint, but needed to pull herself together. She was a mother. And she needed to get home to her son. To Adam.

"I think that ship has sailed," Lewis said, searching the pile of treasure beyond the steps. "But, we might be able to use that." He pointed to the diving suit at the base of the stair. "You can use *etemmu* to heal. So you'll take the oxygen and then heal me as we ascend."

"I have to go into a trance, Lewis. I can't do that while we're swimming for our lives."

The first octopus reached a tentacle into the rising water and let it drift like a person putting their hand out the car window. They definitely were no longer welcome in Ganzir.

"You're going to have to. Look, it's the difference between being a doctor in the hospital and a doctor in the field. I know the thought scares you, but the alternative is that we both drown and stay in this creepy temple forever."

Rachel took a deep breath and nodded.

Lewis took a similar deep breath and stepped outside the temple, swimming down to the suit and removing the oxygen tank. He got the full-face diving mask on and then twisted something on the oxygen tank. He gave a thumb's up to Rachel as he shrugged into the harness and came up to the palace.

He reached for her hand, but his stopped at an invisible point.

Rachel looked behind her at the throne room, checked the water that was now up to her knees. Once she stepped away like Lewis had, there was no return. She looked up. It was so far to the surface.

Impatient, Lewis waved his hand at her. Right. No time like the present.

She closed her eyes and imagined a healing energy until her hands tingled. Then she stepped through into the water. Lewis placed the mask on her as they pushed away from the steps. She closed her eyes and held onto his back, pushing her energy into him. She breathed the oxygen and then sent it into him through *etemmu*. Again and again she breathed for both of them.

And then, as his swimming faltered, Rachel opened her eyes and saw the leaves on the surface. She kicked as hard as she could, bringing his head out of the water.

The current pushed them away from the bridge.

Overhead, Caesar whined. His claws scratched at the limestone as if he wanted to jump down and protect his master.

Rachel held onto Lewis with one arm and grabbed the leaves with the other, holding against the current. Then she gave one last lunge and her hand connected to the arch's platform.

Caesar launched himself from the bridge, landing beside her. The wolf grabbed Captain Lewis's shirt between his teeth and pulled while Rachel pushed from in the water. When he was out, Rachel pulled herself up and turned him onto his side. She continued pushing *etemmu* into him until Lewis sputtered and water flew out of his mouth.

Then she flopped onto her back.

They stayed there until Lewis said it was time to go. He stood up, slowly, and moved to examine the bridge's construction for toe holds. "Let's get to the third gate and we'll set up camp. Hopefully that'll be far enough away that Ereshkigal will forget about us."

"Who was that?" Rachel asked.

"Who was who?"

"The blond woman with the sad eyes."

Captain Lewis shook his head. "I don't know who you mean." He knelt and cupped his hands as a lift for Rachel to climb the short distance from platform up to bridge. "It couldn't have been important."

SWAN DIVE

The serpent rose up, its triangular head over Leda's, swaying. Its mouth opened and she could smell the poison—an evil sweetness—that coated the fangs. The poison it wanted to inject into the eggs.

Swan Dive

*L*eda floated on her back in the water, her swollen belly a giant pearl, and stroked the skin stretched tight over the treasures inside.

"I'll protect you," she promised, but water covered her ears and distorted the sound. She pressed with her fingertips to decipher head or foot or butt. Harder when two babies fought for space. One was vigorous, all flailing elbows while the other pressed back in response, Leda imagined, hands against the belly from the inside. Being in the water like this made Leda feel beautiful. Her dark hair spread through the water and her brown arms and legs were strong, though her middle was round. Someone else had found her beautiful and that errant thought made her cheeks flush as she sat up in the water. These were King Tyndareus's children. That was true enough for the oracle of Delphi to attest, but she kept her gaze from flicking to the chest at the base of her bed.

"Your majesty, it's time to come out before you catch cold." Maybe the words could be considered caring, but the tone was nothing but patronizing.

The older woman was called Nurse—her position for the king decades ago. She wore two shawls at once, had a puckered expression like she drank lemon juice, and insisted that pregnancy must make Leda cold. And that carrying the king's twins meant that Leda shouldn't pick up a sword any longer, even to practice. Or eat anything too spicy because it might hurt the babies.

Leda clenched her fists. It was bad enough that as a princess her father had considered her a pawn to be used in marriage for domestic relations, an object to assure borders would remain intact. Then she was a symbol for the people: look at our glorious queen who participated in the Spartan trials, tamed by King Tyndareus. Now she was a vessel for the birth of an heir and a spare, still being discussed by others. This was her body and her children. Like her mother, she would protect them, educate them, and put a sword in their hands no matter their gender.

Nurse patted Leda dry with a towel and helped her into a loose gown. They left the personal bathing room and walked across the tiled floor to the queen's bedroom. A bed took up the majority of the room, but a looking glass and chair sat near the door to the palace interior, opposite from the walled-in courtyard and garden. The design was similar to the palace where Leda had grown up.

Nurse parted Leda's hair and then braided each side, pulling it tight at each twist. Leda stroked her belly and did not look at the chest or at the entrance to the courtyard. The moon had risen and the perfume of night flowers—gardenia and evening primrose—flowed into the room on a breeze.

She would not think of it as a message. Irritation built at the thoughts she could not think, the looks she could not spare, the memories that she must not, under any circumstances, remember.

"Hold still," Nurse said. "I'm almost finished making you look like a queen."

Leda met Nurse's eyes in the looking glass. "I am a queen."

"Of course," Nurse dropped her eyes and bowed her head in deference, "I didn't mean—"

"Get out." Nurse reported everything that Leda did to Tyndareus, but Leda had no care tonight. "Send in the musicians to play me to sleep."

Nurse scurried away, no doubt to tattle to anyone willing to listen about the young queen's moodiness.

Leda made sure the heavy castle door was shut and then hurried to the chest, dropping to her knees and raising the lid.

"Hello, darlings." There, nestled among soft blankets, sat two eggs with a swan feather between them. Each was the shade of fresh cream and the size of her palm, although one was larger and the other's oval shape more pronounced. Leda stroked them the way she'd stroked her belly. This was her other set of twins.

Alone, she closed her eyes to revisit a moment in the courtyard; the phantom brush of swan feathers across the back of her neck. A bird's trumpeting had snapped her attention from smelling the potted lemon trees to the blue sky. The swan pulled in his wings and plummeted toward the walled-in courtyard. Seconds from crashing, the white bird swept his wings open to slow his descent and landed in Leda's arms, wings hugging her body. There was a moment when she held a bird, proudly arched neck, black mask, webbed feet.

And then his body was shifting, changing, the legs reaching to the ground, the human face emerging from the feathers, arms that wore feathers like a cape still encircling her. Leda was tall, but he stood taller. She was beautiful, but he was impossible. She was made of earth and water, but he was stars and lightning.

Zeus.

"May I?" he asked, dark eyes searching hers.

She understood that he was asking permission. That he would leave if she shook her head. He admired her body—yes, that was clear—but he gave her a choice of whether to accept his attentions. Unlike her father who bartered her for borders or her husband who would visit her bedroom again tonight because it was his duty to father heirs.

"Yes," she whispered. Maybe it would have been impossible to say no to a god, but she didn't want to try.

With a squeak, the interior door swung open. Leda covered the eggs and slammed the lid closed, whirling to scold the musicians for daring to enter without waiting for permission. Instead, an enormous serpent's head pushed through the opening and tasted the air with its tongue.

Eyes wide, Leda kept one hand under her belly and backed around the bed, placing the furniture between herself and the monster. Her sword hung on the wall, a decoration now. The door to the courtyard was on the wall in the other direction. The serpent glided all the way into the bedroom.

Its body was thick as a tree—Leda might be able to touch her fingers together if she hugged it—and as long as the tallest soldier in Sparta's army. A distinctive mix of grey, brown, and black scales covered the body, topped by a triangular head with eyes like onyx. A Milos viper. Venom glistened on its fangs as it reared back its head, searching for her.

"Guards," she screamed.

Heart beating against her ribcage, Leda measured the distance to the courtyard. She'd be trapped within the outside walls, but she could push the bench against the opening to give enough time for the guards to appear. They should be here, rushing in wearing their protective leather armor and carrying their Spartan swords and pikes.

The serpent looked at her and then turned its head away. Its gaze fastened on the chest at the foot of the bed. Intent, it slithered forward, body creating s-shapes as it moved.

"No." The monster wasn't here for her; it was for the babies. This was a fiend sent by a god. Or goddess. And that meant no guards were coming. No help from anyone. Leda turned away from the safety of the courtyard entrance and ran toward the sword on the wall, jerking it from its hooks.

The weight of the sword was familiar, but her body was different, unbalanced. Her calluses had sloughed off in the long baths she'd taken to get relief from an aching lower back and the joint pain from carrying twins. No matter. Her muscles had memory, knew the drills she'd performed over and over.

Leda rushed around the corner of the bed to confront the serpent, but it had reached the chest. It swung its head like a battering ram against the wood. Adjusting her stance to accommodate for her belly, Leda swung the sword down at an angle so it sliced across the tail.

The serpent whipped around as green ichor flowed from the gash.

"Now I have your attention," Leda said. Her heart beat fast, but not with fear. Excitement. The rightness of protecting her babies.

The serpent rose up, its triangular head over Leda's, swaying. Its mouth opened and she could smell the poison—an evil sweetness—that coated the fangs. The poison it wanted to inject into the eggs. Leda sank back into her heels and gripped her sword with both hands.

The serpent lunged and Leda thrust up with the sword, the blade biting through the vulnerable skin, piercing the roof of the mouth, and burying it the reptile's brain. Leda twisted the sword and then moved to the side as the heavy body fell to the floor.

Metal clinked as the scales flipped over until nothing remained but a golden bracelet in the shape of a snake.

Leda touched the trunk where the serpent had battered its head against the wood. It hadn't been able to get inside because it had no hands, but how had it opened the door then?

Whirling to her feet, Leda watched as hands appeared from the air and brought down the edges of a cloak. Everything covered by the cloak remained invisible. Still, the face was enough to identify the intruder. Black hair hung in curls with purple highlights and a pale face with rose red lips created a regal expression. Hera, Queen of the Olympians.

"All these toys and I still have to do it myself."

Leda swallowed. "Toys?"

"The bracelet from Hephaestus and this cloak borrowed from Hermes."

Her sword was no match against Hera. Leda let it fall from her hand and dropped into a curtsy.

"Ha," Hera's laugh was bitter. "You dare pretend to show me respect now."

Leda kept her gaze on the tiled floor. Everyone knew Hera was the goddess of marriage, yet her husband made a fool of her over and over with anyone, mortal or immortal, who caught his eye. Hera's wrath when Zeus fathered Hercules by the mortal Alcmene was legendary. She'd sent snakes to kill Hercules as a baby, too. That hadn't worked either. Maybe her children had a chance.

"Did you know?" Hera walked over to the snake bracelet and picked it up.

Leda came out of the curtsy and walked over to the table where a flagon of wine and two goblets rested. They were always set up in case Tyndareus wanted refreshment.

"Would you care for a drink?" Leda offered. She poured, glad when her hand only shook a little, and then poured one for herself.

Leda waited until Hera sank into a chair before sitting down as well, grateful for the manners her mother had made her learn. A queen must know how to fight with words, too, she'd said.

"Did you?" Hera repeated. Her dark eyebrows arched over blue eyes that held mysteries of Olympus. This was no mortal woman. It wasn't the elegance of her bearing or the uncanny grace of every movement; instead, it was the aura of power. This goddess, daughter of Titans, was here for revenge.

"Not at first." Leda rubbed her neck where swan feathers had caressed. "But, yes, I knew before he kissed me."

Hera's hand closed around the goblet and she brought it up, her throat moving as she swallowed the entire thing and slammed it on the table. "But you let him anyway."

Leda poured another glass for her.

"And now you wait for his children to hatch. You know they will be divine. Is that what you wanted? Is that why you enticed him?"

Leda heard the rage underlying the accusation. This was like a swordfight. She had to make a perfect move against a stronger opponent. For now, she twisted the stem of the goblet between her thumb and index finger.

"I should make you writhe with pain for your adultery. I am the goddess of marriage and you made a mockery of marriages in general and mine specifically."

Hera's face was ethereal; it couldn't be unlovely. But... Leda recognized a sadness in the expression, almost invisible lines of pain etched across her forehead.

"I'm sorry. I didn't think of you," Leda said, meaning it. In trying to rebel against her own restraints, she'd hurt a woman, a wife. She opened herself to attack by being vulnerable and then adopted a defensive stance. "But please don't punish my babies. You are also the goddess of childbirth."

"Aren't you clever to use my own loyalties against me." Hera took another sip.

Leda cleared her throat. "I'm a mortal. I'm no comparison to you."

"That's true." Hera's gaze rested on the chest with the eggs.

Leda searched for an argument, something to convince the goddess not to exact revenge.

"My husband can be very persuasive when he wants someone."

Unsure of whether this was a trap to make Leda claim to be a victim, she said, "I can only speak for myself. Please forgive me." Leda bowed her head.

Hera snorted.

The sound from the regal woman was so unlikely that Leda had to look up.

"You are only a mortal and this is your first offense." Hera gave her a rueful half-smile. "I suppose I could have taken this problem to my husband instead of hunting you down."

"Men are celebrated for breaking the rules, but women are hated," Leda said, trying to build a relationship with the goddess.

Hera twisted the stem of the goblet. "Are you hated?"

"I would be, if Tyndareus told the people I was unfaithful."

"Ah." Hera took a sip. "And how are you going to explain four children?"

"I keep thinking about it." Leda shook her head. "Nurse will be in the birthing chamber. She'll tell Tyndareus everything."

"Advice from one queen to another." Hera pointed a finger at Leda. "You must surround yourself with women you can trust. A circle of friends is more valuable than ambrosia."

The interior door flew open. Tyndareus appeared in the doorway, guards behind and, yes, there was Nurse peeking through too.

"I was in the council chamber and we heard you call for help." Tyndareus had the golden skin and average build of men in Sparta. He was an academic with his facial hair groomed into a point and soft hands. He examined the room.

Leda saw the soft glimmer that meant Hera had pulled up the edges of Hermes's invisibility cloak. The serpent was gone, back in the bracelet around Hera's arm. There was nothing to see in the bed chamber.

"Merely a nightmare, my lord," Leda said. "I thought intruders had attacked."

"We need to change her diet," Nurse said, clucking her tongue.

The king nodded. "Do that immediately, Nurse."

"I don't think—" Leda said.

"Maybe a guard outside her door?" Nurse asked.

"Not necessary." Leda noticed her sword still on the floor. "I'm fine."

"Excellent plan. I'll assign a guard." The king clapped Nurse's shoulder as if she were a soldier. "I don't know what I'd do without you."

The door was pulled shut and Leda was locked inside with a dangerous goddess. It was almost enough to make her laugh.

Hera pulled the cloak's hood down. "You have no power here."

"Tyndareus doesn't care about me at all. Only for the two babies that he fathered."

"Your marriage is unhappy, Leda. He is not a strong enough partner for you." Hera tapped a finger against the wine goblet. "I may have acted impetuously when I sent the serpent to attack the children you conceived with Zeus."

That was the closest the goddess would approach an apology to a mortal. Leda shrugged as if the concession wasn't shocking.

"I took care of it."

"That was very impressive to watch, actually." Hera smiled, her entire face lighting up.

"Thank you." Leda had to blink the radiance away or she would sit there admiring the goddess for an eternity.

"It explains why your children are special," Hera said. "All four of them."

"They are everything to me." Leda met Hera's eyes and did not soften her tone. "I will protect them with my life."

Hera waved a hand, the garnet ring sparkling. "They are everything to you because you are their mother. Am I not the goddess of birth? Do I not understand the sacred bond between a mother and her baby?"

Leda put the goblet to her mouth to keep from pointing out that Hera had tried to murder her children earlier this evening.

"No, I mean your children are special to everyone. But you. The oracle did not say what happens to you."

Leda controlled her expression. Hera knew more than she'd let on. If the children were special, then Hera couldn't kill them. It would defy the fates and those three crones wouldn't allow that. And tonight was a liminal space if her own fate couldn't be read.

"Have you chosen names?"

Leda rubbed her belly. "I believe I'm carrying a boy and a girl. Tyndareus and I chose the names: Castor and Clytemnestra."

Hera nodded as if she recognized the names.

"And the other twins?"

"I haven't chosen yet. Would you honor us by naming them?"

Hera tapped her garnet ring, but her gaze was unfocused. The air grew close, heavy with possibility. It was time for Leda's final move.

"You are the goddess of marriage and childbirth." Leda swallowed. "I petition for your help and I make an offering in exchange."

Hera's attention returned to the sleeping chamber. She raised an eyebrow.

"Intriguing. Most people go through my priestesses or at least travel to my temple. Where is the altar, Leda?"

"Fortune brought you to me instead." It was a daring comment and Leda wondered if she'd been too familiar with the queen, but Hera laughed.

"Fine, my fellow queen. Ask me your petition and if it is within my power, I will grant it on this strange night."

Thoughts swirled, but Leda mastered them, pushed them into an order that would make sense.

"I need help in the birthing room so that all four of my children may be accepted as Tyndareus's children until they are grown and their divine origins revealed. This will help me as their mother and it will help the world because you said they each have a role to play. In exchange, I sacrifice myself to you. When my children are grown, I will serve in your circle of women on Olympus and protect you with my sword and with my words, with my heart and with my mind."

If Hera would accept this then Leda could accept a loveless marriage and Nurse's hovering and all the other entrapments of being a woman who represented power but had very little.

Hera stood up and looked into the walled-in courtyard.

"Why should I trust you? Perhaps you want to sleep with my husband again. Maybe you yearn for eternal life."

"You have seen the truth of my marriage as I have seen yours. I will not cross another woman ever again." Leda pressed her palms together and bowed her head. "I ask my petition from one queen to another."

Hera paced the room until she stopped in front of the chest and opened it. She caressed one egg and then the other with her index finger.

Leda held her breath and clenched her fists against her instinct to stand in front of the chest.

"This one shall be called Pollux and the girl shall be called Helen—they'll call her 'of Troy'." The goddess nodded and pivoted to face Leda. "I accept your offer. No one can know of our agreement or it will be of little use. You will be my spy on earth and then on Olympus. Your loyalty will be to me and I will watch over you and your children."

Hera held up the swan feather that nestled with the eggs and she pulled along the quill so that the white turned to turquoise and an eye pattern formed at the tip. Hera placed the peacock feather in the trunk before bringing the cloak up and gliding out into the night.

Leda sank down with her back against the bed, one hand under her belly and one hand on her eggs. Yes, she'd have an unending life of being a servant on Olympus, but if she could negotiate with the queen of the gods, then the guard outside her door and overbearing Nurse had no chance of controlling her. A flutter of motion from her belly as one baby kicked against her palm at the same time an egg rocked.

"Hush, children. Mother will take care of you."

An Excuse, An Invitation Even

Eunice heard the music before she rounded the bend and saw the broken-down stagecoach with the name ARGO painted in glossy black across the back. Nearby, two horses stood in the creek—one favoring his back leg, while a man, shoes off and trousers rolled up, sat on a flat rock and strummed a lyre. After riding over seventy-five miles for the mail route, Eunice wanted nothing more than to feed Doc and fall into bed. But the notes of the song beckoned, making her forget the exhaustion that clouded her mind. Eunice clucked to Doc and rubbed his neck. Like many of the horses for the Western route, Doc was a Mustang, compact and sure-footed. Eunice adjusted her position in the saddle, touched the handle of her revolver, and urged Doc forward.

"Hello." The man set aside the lyre and stood. "My name's Orpheus."

He was tall with broad shoulders, a handsome face with arresting blue eyes, dark hair cut short, and brown skin complemented by a white shirt, trousers, and a fashionable overcoat with wide lapels. A pocket watch hung on a chain from his vest, glinting golden in the spring sun. His hands had long fingers with clean nails. So. The stranger was wealthy and not used to physical work.

Narrowing her eyes, Eunice pieced together what had happened. The embankment had softened after the spring rains. The weight of the stagecoach collapsed the ground. As the stagecoach fell it would have pulled on the harnessed horses and caused them to panic.

"Why are you playing songs when your coach is broken?"

"I thought perhaps the fish would leap onto the rock and I would have a meal."

Did he have sunstroke or did he think this was charming?

"Are the wheels intact?" Eunice dismounted and looped the reins. Taking off her sombrero, she squinted against the sunshine: there was no shade on the Great Plains.

"I believe so. It's about time to replace the steel rim, but I haven't been near a blacksmith." He was matter-of-fact. As if he had no worries about being stranded overnight.

"Hmmm." She waded into the creek and approached the Morgan first. She whispered to him until his ears twitched and then laid a hand on his shoulder. He swung his head to her and blew out a breath. "That's a good one," she crooned. He was in good condition, well-fed and no scars. The assessment of an animal was an assessment of the man.

Eunice moved to the Thoroughbred.

"Careful. He's dangerous."

"Not to me." She smiled, though her back was to Orpheus. "I have a way with horses."

Eunice hummed as she slid her hand down his leg, noting the warmth near the fetlock. She squeezed and he responded to the cue, lifting his foot. Running her fingers in the track along the frog, Eunice found a deep cut. Probably from one of the sharp creek stones when the coach slipped. She released the hoof and stared down at the water, thinking.

Music notes floated into a tune that Eunice almost recognized. Pleasant with a hint of melancholy, dipping into a minor key and back again. This wasn't her problem, but the only way to survive out here was to look after one another. It was already mid-afternoon. Slim chance that anyone else would come by to offer help.

"You'll have to come to the station," she said, turning to face Orpheus. "Doc and I will lead the way. We'll go slow."

"That's very kind. I would like to thank you properly," he said, eyes laughing as if they shared a joke, "but I'd need to know your name first."

"Eunice." She swallowed, his teasing sparking a nervous excitement that took her by surprise. To cover it, she added, "I'm only helping because of your horse. I feel pain when an animal is hurt."

"You are a sensitive woman," he said, plucking a melody from the lyre. "I admire that."

The ride to the station felt much longer than it was and, though she refused to glance back, she couldn't shake that feeling that he was smiling at her the whole way.

The Pony Express station was actually an abandoned military outpost: two main buildings in the middle, a stable and round pen to one side and a set of barracks on the other. A rough fence encircled the entirety. The door to the main building on the left, nicknamed 'The House', opened and Dog, a shaggy Heeler, bounded down the steps. Mrs. Nimea followed right after. The woman and her husband had immigrated from Greece decades ago and then Mr. Nimea had died. Now Mrs. Nimea worked as station master: communicating with the other outposts, arranging riders' schedules, and sharing the horse care.

"This is Orpheus," Eunice said. "He needs a place to stay until his horse heals and he can get someone to look at a wheel."

Orpheus took off his hat and swept into a bow. "Thank you for your hospitality."

His voice was smooth as molasses, deep as a pond, as moving as dawn sweeping across the Plains.

"How delightful to have a guest." Nimea clasped her hands together like a schoolgirl though she was in her mid-50's. "Eunice, why don't you show Orpheus the stable and then come in and help me with the meal?"

Eunice led Doc into the stable and put him on cross ties to take off his saddle. The empty mochila, crafted to hold the mail, was hung on a hook. Then she took off the sombrero and shook out her straight reddish-blond hair. She had sweat marks across her forehead like Doc had sweat marks where the girth had been. Eunice used the water from a bucket to wash her face and hands until Orpheus entered, holding each of his horses by the halter.

"Which stall?" His jacket was off and his sleeves rolled up to expose his forearms.

Pushing wet hair behind her ears, Eunice motioned to the empty ones.

"Thrace is a good horse. Do you think he'll recover?"

"Pass me the gauze behind you." She stepped into the stall and cued Thrace to lift his hoof. She washed the cut and spread a salve before wrapping the gauze over and under. "Yes, but he'll need rest."

"You're good with animals."

"I am." It was an acknowledgement rather than a boast. "They're honest. You can't have a partnership without trust and you can't have trust without honesty."

Eunice patted Thrace's shoulder as Orpheus moved aside so she could leave the stall. Moving past him she caught a hint of cologne and underneath that something like cedar. Fresh, clean, and a little sharp. Enticing. Like she should turn around and kiss him.

Instead, Eunice walked inside the house and smelled hard biscuits baking. Nimea already had boiled eggs, beans, and dried fruit ready. Most noteworthy, Nimea had changed into her Sunday best, a dress that hugged her generous curves, and had her dark hair pinned up.

"You don't need my help," Eunice said, confused.

"No. Instead, I'm helping you. Don't you read the newspapers you deliver? That's the musician Orpheus. He was part of the crew who reclaimed the gold stolen by the gang posing as shepherds buying land. The newspapers called it 'The Golden Fleecing.'"

"How'd they get the gold?"

"I only read above the fold and it was a long article." Nimea put her hands on her hips. "The point is that he's a famous hero. You're a legend of the Pony Express. It's meant to be."

"Is matchmaking part of your station duties?"

"Maybe." Nimea jabbed her finger in the air. "Now go change out of those stinky clothes. The prairie is magnificent tonight so we'll eat outside. He'll play music; there will be dancing." She put her arms around an invisible partner and twirled around the kitchen.

Eunice sighed. "He's not from here and I'm not leaving my horses. I belong here, to the land."

"Gracious, girl, that's a fine way to put the cart before the horse." Nimea did one more pirouette and then sagged against the wall, fanning herself. "Stop thinking so hard about the future and enjoy the present. Talk to the man before you decide if you want to get closer. And if not, then you had a good time. And if you do, well, go after what you want."

It made sense. Why not enjoy a night of music and dancing with a handsome man? Eunice went to her room and straight to the closet to pull out a dress. She'd bought it without any occasion in mind because it was so pretty. She ran her fingers over the deep blue calico. The color made her think of Orpheus's eyes.

Nimea knocked and then opened the door without waiting for an answer. "I brought warm water."

Hurrying, Eunice shrugged off her dirty clothes, bathed, and pulled on clean chemise and pantalets.

"This fits you perfectly." Nimea adjusted the dress. "Let me fix your hair and you'll be beautiful. No time for curls, but I'll braid and pin."

✻

Outside, Orpheus had arranged the dining table and chairs. Food was laid out like a church potluck. Broad strokes of pinks, purples, and peach painted the sky.

Orpheus sat near the fire pit playing tug-of-war with Dog.

"We have arrived." Nimea posed in the doorway.

Orpheus smiled as he stood up. "My hostess is a jewel of the Pony Express station."

Giggling, Nimea stepped aside.

But when Eunice stepped forward, Orpheus's smiled wavered.

Heat swept from her chest to her face. Was something wrong with the way she looked?

Without dropping his gaze, Orpheus stepped around Dog and stopped at the bottom of the steps, bowing at the waist before straightening. Flustered, Eunice dropped into a curtsy. He extended his hand and she took it as she walked down the steps.

Gleeful, Nimea said, "Will you bless the food, Orpheus?"

"I pray for the sun that nourishes the soil; I pray for the food that feeds our bodies. I thank God for poetry that nourishes our imaginations and music that feeds our souls. Amen."

Eyes closed, Eunice swayed to the rhythm of Orpheus's words, the reverent tone in his voice. When it was over, she blinked to see they were still outside, the sun at the horizon.

"Where is your family, Orpheus?" Nimea asked, passing out plates.

"My father, Dr. Apollo, is retired from teaching at university in Greece and escorts my mother, Calliope, wherever she wants to go."

Eunice's eyes widened. "Your mother is Calliope? The singer who travels to the capitals of Europe?"

"My mother is a famous woman," Orpheus said, raising his eyebrows, "but I didn't know her reputation stretched to the Great Plains of America."

"We get the news out here because I deliver it." Despite Nimea's accusation, Eunice did look over the newspapers and had seen the photos of Orpheus's parents: his father dressed in expensive suits and his mother wearing jewelry that queens couldn't afford. No wonder he was used to bowing and all the civilized manners.

"I also didn't know that women rode for the Pony Express." He spread butter on a hard biscuit. "I wouldn't have expected to find that."

"Because women are too fragile?" She lifted her chin. "I earned the position."

The butter knife slid from his grip to the grass as Orpheus tried to explain. "I—"

Eunice held up her fingers with each point.

"Riders can't weigh more than 125 pounds. Riders have to be expert. And willing to risk death. I'm part of the reason that letters from St. Joseph, Missouri to Sacramento, California are delivered in ten days. In exchange I get almost $100 per month." She lowered her hand. "Out here, in the West, rules aren't as important as who can do the job."

"Riding for the Pony Express is impressive." Orpheus leaned forward. "And I agree about the opportunities in America's West. That's one of the reasons I love visiting here."

Dog jumped up from his place by Orpheus and growled, staring into the distance.

"That must be Mr. Arist. He's a rancher who rents the other building and comes over for supper sometimes," Nemia explained.

"Or it could be Mr. Highman, the traveling preacher. He's supposed to come tomorrow, though."

"It's Arist." Eunice said. "I can tell by Dog's reaction."

The rancher stepped around the corner of the building. He was thick around the middle and had a ruddy complexion. It was spring but he hadn't shaved his winter beard yet.

"Meet our guest, Orpheus. He's a musician," Nimea said. "We're about to have coffee and then I will implore Orpheus to play for us."

"Musician? That's not a real job." Arist piled food onto his plate. "I'm out there moving cattle around to provide food for people. Can't live without food."

"In answer I would paraphrase a teacher who said humans do not live by bread alone, but are spiritual beings." Orpheus smiled. "But I also would add that stories—spoken or sung—give us reason for our existence. Art, indeed, reveals how to surrender to life and engage with every moment—painful or joyful—as a gift."

Eunice's shoulders relaxed. That was it. That was how she felt when riding in partnership with a horse, whether galloping across the flat or loosening the reins and squeezing with her legs as they jumped a fallen obstacle.

"If you'll excuse me, dear Nimea," Orpheus said, standing, "I'll retrieve my lyre from the barracks."

She waved him away.

Arist didn't wait to attack. "Orpheus? What the hell kind of name is that? Sounds like orifice."

"It's Greek," Nimea said, tone icy. "Same as mine."

Eunice stood up to clear the table, annoyed. Arist was so crass.

"Is that fancy boy why you're all dressed up?" Arist asked Eunice. "You've never done that for me."

"Aren't you acting jealous," Nimea scolded. Then, joining Eunice at the table, Nimea lowered her voice. "Arist seems to think that he has a claim on you."

Eunice shook her head. "I've given him no encouragement."

"I see the way he looks at you." Nimea picked up two glasses. "Beware."

By the time the supper dishes had been tidied, Arist had a fire started and the stars had come out with spring constellations twinkling overhead. Orpheus stood with one leg propped on a log to support a lyre.

Eunice relaxed into her chair, wine glass in her hand, fire sending warmth to her feet and wind stroking her hair. Orpheus played the lyre and she didn't know whether she preferred when he was vulnerable, his attention on the strings, or when he looked at her as he sang, making it personal. At some point she realized that Arist left and then a hand squeezed her shoulder and Nimea was gone as well. Lightning bugs came out—first of the season—flashing their messages of love as accompaniment to Orpheus's song.

Eunice set the wine glass on the ground—noticing it was still full. Not the reason, then, for her desire. As if it were a signal, his fingers stilled on the lyre's strings.

"Will you walk with me?" he asked. "Show me this wild place you call home."

She nodded and stood.

He offered his arm. "It is an excuse, an invitation even, for you to touch me," he whispered, "I know you do not need my support."

He'd taken off his jacket while playing and had his sleeves rolled up the way he had in the stable. Eunice let her fingers hover over his bare skin, ready to swear she felt heat, before lowering them down. They walked toward the gate to the road. Between the waxing moon and the lightning bugs, there was enough light for her sneak glances at his profile.

"Stay on the road," she said. "Snakes will be waking up this time of year."

"Then you'd have to save me again. I'm not sure my confidence could withstand such an assault."

She laughed and turned to him. "I like you a great deal."

"And I like you, little mustang."

Her lips twitched. "Little mustang?"

"Is there anything more fitting? At first meeting you are a wild spirit on a horse, an image of the Great Plains sent to rescue me from my own folly. Then you emerge from the house the equal to any beauty in a European court. There is no situation that defeats you. Indeed, I would be glad of you as a companion in all of my travels."

She shook her head, but wanted to believe. "Those are fancy words."

"May I show you what I mean?"

She nodded and closed her eyes as he bent down to touch his lips to hers.

He started to straighten, to break off the kiss, but Eunice held onto his shoulders and pulled him back down. His hands came around her waist. Yes, she wanted this man who played music and spoke philosophy and understood that she had many facets.

And when this kiss ended, the stars wheeled overhead and she had to hold onto him or she would fall. Or maybe she was already falling.

"I ride for the Pony Express."

"Yes, I know." He was laughing, but it wasn't mean. "And I'm a music man. But those are details that will hang off of whatever we decide. If we are together, then we are enough for anything."

"You must be honest with me."

"I will tell you everything; I will bare myself to you as I have to no one before you."

"Then I will walk with you to the ends of the earth." She interlaced her fingers with his.

They settled into chairs to talk through the night, stopping to kiss when the words ran dry. Sometimes Orpheus would get up to put another log on the fire and sometimes Eunice would. Soon after false dawn, Eunice drifted to sleep in the chair.

She woke to Arist leaning over her, eyes bloodshot and breath smelling of whiskey. Glancing to the other chair, it was empty.

"You little slut," Arist slurred. "I'll tell everyone what you've done."

She ducked her head to get away. The early sun glinted on something metal in the grass. The butter knife from the evening before.

"Where's Orpheus?" Eunice leaned so that her fingers touched the ground. "What did you do to him?"

"Didn't do anything." He grabbed her cheek. "Fancy boy ran away after using you. Like a steer with a cow."

There! Grasping the handle of the knife, she plunged the blade into Arist's leg.

With a yowl of pain, Arist straightened and Eunice lunged to her feet, running for the house. He stumbled after her, grabbing her dress. It ripped.

"Let me go," Eunice said, hating that her voice shook.

"Whore," Arist said. He grabbed her arm and pushed her toward the ground.

Nimea yanked open the door, standing in the doorway wearing a nightgown and pointing a Henry rifle. "I do not miss." Dog stood beside her, growling.

Arist's grip tightened before he thrust Eunice away.

"Get out of here," Nimea hollered.

Eunice stumbled up the stairs and collapsed onto the porch.

Shuffling into a run, Arist disappeared around the building. Teeth bared, Dog charged after him.

Still cradling the rifle, Nimea dropped to her knees. "Are you hurt?"

Eunice wrapped her arms around herself. She couldn't stop shaking.

A horse whinnied from the road.

"That's Doc," Nimea said squinting.

"It's Orpheus," Eunice said. Energy rushed through her frozen limbs and she stood, holding onto the post.

"But there's a man sitting behind him." Nimea touched her haircap. "It's Mr. Highman."

"Highman," Eunice repeated. Orpheus hadn't left her. He'd gone to get the traveling preacher.

"I never," Nimea said. "They're about to see my nightclothes."

"Go inside." Eunice straightened. "I'm recovered."

Doc jogged through the fence and up to the main building.

"Morning, little mustang." Orpheus dismounted. "I couldn't wait another minute for our wedding."

"I have spent the ride trying to convince Mr. Orpheus that this is not a good idea. You two have just met." Mr. Highman cleared his throat. "However, I've been convinced otherwise."

Orpheus winked. Ahh. He paid off the preacher. His expression grew concerned. "What's wrong?"

"Nothing, now."

Orpheus moved forward until it felt like they were alone. "Tell me later?"

"Yes." She leaned against her partner.

"I love you," Orpheus pledged. "In this life and the next."

The door opened and Nimea emerged, dressed. "We'll have the wedding as soon as we gather something old, something new, something borrowed, something blue." She rubbed her hands together. "Father, is it too early for a glass of wine?"

"Generally, I would say decorum must prevail, but as I've spent the last two hours riding a horse, my throat *is* a bit parched."

"I love you," Eunice pledged, still in the protective embrace of Orpheus's arms. "In this life and the next."

WHERE THE KELPIES SWIM

*Ghost's little white head bobbed in the moonlight, his sharp baby teeth
exposed as if that would scare away the monster.*

Where the Kelpies Swim

*A*cross the bay, the herd of water horses galloped straight from their island into the waves, fearless. Muscles bunched under smooth skin, sharp teeth bared in eagerness, fins fluttered along their legs. Watching the animals made Hali's chest ache with longing. Jealousy and admiration twined together inside her. They were so beautiful and fierce and she...was not. Soon only their heads and necks were visible; the kelpies had started their Annual Swim from Nursery Island to the main barrier island. Each mare had a smaller yearling swimming beside her. One Johnnie—soldiers who rode the kelpies against the sea monsters who lived beyond the islands—led the herd on a black stallion and another on a black-and-white paint brought up the rear. The Johnnies ignored the audience watching from the beach. They always did. Even though they fought to keep the Mainlanders safe, no Mainlanders were allowed on the Barrier Islands that stretched across the mouth of the wide bay. Occasionally, the news networks tried to send a journalist to investigate the rumors of telepathic bonds between the riders and their kelpies. The Johnnies never let the journalists dock, though, and no Mainlander wanted to be floating indefinitely in the water where every moment that passed brought a higher chance of a sea monster attack. Hali shivered at the thought.

Tourists crowded the beach to watch the Swim and one of them elbowed Hali in the ribs. She frowned up at him, knowing he wouldn't pay attention. She was small for her age, sixteen, with average brown hair and plain features. More than that, she wore the uniform of a resort worker. That made her invisible to the tourists—until they needed their drink refreshed.

Hali shifted in the crowd to see better. The water horses were all different shades: bays and chestnuts, grays and paints. As the Swim reached the halfway mark, the herd passed in front of the beach. Water smacked and splashed as the horses' heads jutted forward in rhythm, their limbs churning underneath the water and creating a white froth. In front, the black stallion's mane cascaded down like wild, tangled seaweed. He lifted his head and nickered a challenge into the air. His rider rubbed his neck in a familiar motion and a flicker lit up along the stallion's neck in faint runes. The Mainlander crowd exhaled in a mix of envy and yearning. Gradually Hali recognized a familiar buzzing sound from above the crowd. A network drone hovered as it recorded the Swim. Suddenly the drone darted forward over the water toward the herd. Someone nearby gasped. Whoever was directing the drone was breaking the unspoken rule that defined the space between Johnnies and Mainlanders. A tourist pushed back his hat and said, "That's going to be the shot on all the networks."

The drone flew closer to the herd until it hovered over the waves a hands-width from the churning water. Startled, the mares shied away from the drone and its strange noise, switching into a protective mode and pushing their foals to a safe distance. One mare's eyes rolled as she attempted to rear in the water and instead swam into another mare causing that mare to nip at the original kelpie's flank. The rear Johnnie glared at the tourists on the beach, eyebrows furrowed over her blue eyes. Without any command that Hali could see, the Johnnie's paint kelpie launched from the water, her mouth opened wide to expose large, pointed teeth. Teeth that belonged to a predator. She crunched the drone between her jaws, dragging it down as she submerged. A moment later the Johnnie and the kelpie emerged, water sluicing off as both shook their heads. Excited screams erupted along the beach. Some people even clapped at the spectacle. Without a backwards glance at the tourists, the rear rider swam to catch up to the scattered herd.

As far as the tourists were concerned, the Annual Swim was over. Music blasted from speakers set up at the corner of Dearie's restaurant, the place where Hali worked. The smells of grilled meat and fruity drinks drifted into the air. No one watched the water horses anymore; instead, the tourists would return to their homes talking about the vicious, unruly creatures. Heart thumping, Hali pushed through the edges of the crowd and walked south along the beach toward the driftwood that marked the edge of restaurant territory. Finding a larger piece, Hali settled on the driftwood. She, at least, would watch the end of the Swim.

As if in answer, a beep on her wrist comm followed by a mild shock pulse informed her she was late for work. The comm, obviously, was the cheap version. Two prongs went straight down from the interface into Hali's arm between radius and ulna and a two-inch-long "tail" underneath inserted into the skin and pointed toward the elbow. Scars had formed years ago, securing it into position. Hali grimaced. If she didn't hurry then her foster mother, Dearie, would increase the electric charge. The Swim attracted a brace of tourists from inland and Dearie counted on the tourists to spend enough for the restaurant to make it through the rest of the year.

Ignoring the comm for a moment, Hali squinted at the largest island. The black stallion emerged onto sand at the mouth of a steep-walled canyon and most of the herd followed, but some kelpies were still circling, looking for their foals. After the drone incident, the orderly pairs of mothers and foals had turned into one overlapping group. As mothers found their foals, they left the water. More Johnnies in their distinctive waterproof brown riding jackets appeared from a gap in the canyon wall to help move the kelpies inland. Hali counted the bobbing heads still in the water. Then, confused, she counted again. It shouldn't be an odd number.

Waves splashed against the beach near Hali's driftwood as if something thrashed in the water. An instinctive ripple of fear shot

173

from Hali's heart to stomach. Mainlanders were taught to stay away from the water and shown grainy photos of the sea monsters. Nicknamed "unseels," shorthand for "undersea eels," they were long—sometimes 20 feet—round, with a membraned dorsal fin, and blind because they lived deep in the ocean. Instead of sight, they depended on sensitivity to the smell of blood in the water to fix on their prey. They attacked from under the water or thrust their long bodies onto land, latched onto prey, and dragged the animal or person back down into the water. The long net, final line of defense between islands and mainland, had to be lowered for the Annual Swim. Red lights now blinked on each mast at the ends of the net as warning for humans not to enter the water.

Had an unseel come in? Or...Hali shaded her eyes.

There! A little white head bobbed in the breakers near the sandbar. Nostrils tinted a delicate pink flared with heavy breathing. One small hoof broke the surface and then the other. The foal must have gotten separated in the chaos with the drone. It was panicking, using up all its strength to stay afloat.

"Hey," Hali yelled. She climbed on the driftwood and waved her arms for attention from the Johnnies. "Back here!"

Bass thumped through the music speakers. No one on the beach could hear her, so there was no way anyone across the bay would be able to. They were too far away.

Riders and water horses were tiny, distant figures, but one kelpie stayed in the surf. The grey mare with white spots and dark mane and tail ran back and forth between the water and shore, screaming in defiance. The rear Johnnie and her paint drove the mare onto land, forcing her back step by step. Then they were gone.

The water horses and Riders had disappeared into the privacy of the island; they'd given up on finding the missing foal.

The yearling's head dipped under the water.

Hali jumped down and paced the shoreline. "Come on," she begged the deity of fortune. "Lady Moon, please help."

Another shock, stronger this time, ripped through Hali's arm from the wrist comm. The comm held all the information of Hali's life: how long she slept, where she was, how much money she still owed to Dearie on her contract. Hali tapped the sensor so it would read her location. That should turn off the alarm for a moment, but Dearie would take away pay since she was supposed to be working.

The foal still hadn't emerged from the water, and she was the only one who knew it was drowning. Regardless of the danger of giant eels, Hali plunged into the water. It was cold; the current that prompted the kelpies to swim came from beyond the archipelago. Hali swam forward, trying to coordinate her limbs and her breath, and paused to tread water. There were pools on the mainland—safe places to play in the water, but never this openness. Never the reality that she wouldn't be able to touch the ground. And she'd covered such a short distance.

There was no bobbing white head. There was nothing out here.

Who am I to think I can rescue a kelpie? Even the Johnnies gave up and they know more about kelpies than I do. A painful current ran from her wrist comm straight up her spine and into her brain, causing an immediate headache. Spots danced in her vision. Dearie was not happy. Then, underneath the artificial headache, came an overwhelming sense of fear and desperation. It bypassed all rational thought, and Hali reacted.

Once again she windmilled her arms through the water and kicked toward the sandbar. No more thoughts of giving up. She needed to help, needed to get to the source of those feelings.

Her feet hit the sandbar even as a thick body in the water barreled into her so they both did a somersault in the water. Reaching out, blinded by the saltwater, Hali felt the solid body of the foal. A spindly leg that looked fragile was still strong enough to strike her and Hali's mouth opened and she choked on saltwater. Bending her knees and pushing off the sand, Hali propelled to the surface and sucked in a breath, one hand still on the foal. Standing on the sandbar with feet spread for stability, Hali moved her hand up the foal's neck to underneath the jaw, being careful of the sharp teeth, and lifted the head from the water.

The foal, scared, didn't seem to realize he could breathe at first. *How did she know it was a he?* Yet, she was certain.

"Calm down with those legs," she said. "You already got me once."

His right eye, a watery shade of gray, rolled to look at her and everything seemed to stop. He was perfect. Up close his coat was

175

pale gray with a hint of future spots. His velvet muzzle fit into the curve of her palm, his shoulders bunched as he moved his legs, and his dark mane grew along his neck in rebellious tufts rather than classic waves. On land his head would reach her chest. That's why she could stand on the sandbar and he couldn't.

A sense of approval washed through her. Gratitude and then so much joy that Hali whimpered with the shock. No one had ever loved her so completely. Somehow, she was communicating with the kelpie, the way the Johnnies did.

Helpless to resist, Hali laughed with joy.

"Ghost. That's what I'm going to call you. Is that okay?"

Questioning.

"You're like me. We're invisible to most people." She tilted her head as she remembered the pacing mare. "But you have someone special and I'm going to get you back to her."

She rubbed along his neck the way she'd seen the Johnnie do. There was a slight tingle—not like the shock that a wrist comm gave, but like a feather brushing over sensitive skin. She had no idea if it would work, but she pictured them standing on shore, together. "I'll be right beside you."

Hali touched Ghost's shoulder with one hand and stepped off the sandbar. Adrenaline gave her a burst of energy and Hali modified a side stroke so she and Ghost wouldn't be separated. Waves pushed them from behind and then pulled at their progress, but touching Ghost kept Hali focused. He needed her.

Soon Ghost's hooves struck sand and he dug in and forward, one last push onto the mainland. Hali glanced toward the beach party, but no had even noticed their struggle. She could have drowned and only Dearie would notice when she didn't show up for work. Pushing those thoughts away in lieu of being grateful that they didn't have an audience, Hali urged Ghost toward the trees.

The colt hung his head. His legs trembled with exhaustion.

"Come on," she said, firm. "No drone is catching sight of you."

Stumbling, Ghost followed her into the trees. His absolute trust made Hali's eyes fill with tears. How could she love him so much already? They moved along a path she'd made years ago. The tourists all stayed at the resorts and all the workers went to other resorts to blow off steam before returning to their own. So this isolated area had become a refuge. She brought Ghost to a lean-to made of three wooden shipping pallets against three sturdy pine trunks.

Ghost's legs folded and he slumped to the ground. His eyes closed. Hali stroked his shoulder, no longer even worrying about his sharp teeth, but he didn't move. Poor baby wasn't waking up for anything.

Hali grabbed a blanket from inside the lean-to and tucked it around the kelpie. As she leaned close to Ghost, she caught a whiff of something sweet. She leaned closer. He smelled warm and a little salty and a little musty like dried summer grass.

Hali broke into a jog, backtracking to the beach so no one wondered why she was coming from the trees. At the largest palm tree Hali slowed down, pressed a hand to the cramp in her side, and veered into Dearie's hotel grounds, resting against the stack of boats and kayaks. It was locked because the nets were down for the Swim. When the nets were up then tourists could paddle around between the surf and the sandbar. If the nets were breached by sea monsters, then the Johnnies would sound an alarm. There would, theoretically, be time to get to safety. Once it would have been unthinkable to go in the water for recreation, but it had been so many years since the nets had been breached that more tourists had grown bold.

A sudden thought made Hali twist around. The lights on the masts still glowed red. The nets were still down. That meant the sea monsters could attack. It meant the Johnnies were still hoping the foal could make it home. Back to his mother. Hali nodded. She was going to make that miracle come true.

"Hey, Moonface! You're late," Roni said, hands on hips. Two years older than Hali, Roni was Dearie's favorite foster. Tonight, she wore a flattering one-shoulder romper. "And why are you wet?"

"I—" Hali searched for anything to say. "I thought if I could get the drone then I could sell it back to the networks for a fortune. I'd be able to pay off my entire contract to Dearie."

"You're an idiot, but that's not a terrible idea." Roni held up the keys attached to her belt. "I'm the assistant tonight so I'll take your fine. One month's wages."

"A whole month?" Hali's stomach dropped. She'd been paying her contract since she was eight years old and was on target to finish on her 17ᵗʰ birthday.

"Then, you'll pull out all the tables and chairs yourself." Roni tilted her head towards Dearie's form moving among the tables of tourists. "Or I'll tell Dearie about your stupid swim. She'll shock you so hard you pass out."

Hali clenched her fists. It was so unfair. Another month added to working at this stupid restaurant. It didn't matter. Hali released her fists and relaxed her shoulders. The only thing that mattered was Ghost. She had to get him home before the nets went up.

Hali lifted her wrist and tapped her wrist comm.

Roni's comm beeped confirmation.

"Hope the unseels don't eat you." Roni called in a sweet voice as she floated toward the guests.

Hali didn't mind doing the tables. She didn't interact with the tourists particularly well because she didn't understand all the social cues that seemed to come to others naturally. She missed out on tourist tips, but tonight it gave her a chance to sneak away. After setting the last chair into place, Hali faced the resort.

While the sun set in brilliant peach and mauve, Roni lit the tiki torches against the darkness. Near the pool cabana Dearie drank with the tourists. All attention would be on squeezing tourists for money. If everyone here passed out by dawn then it would be easy to grab a kayak. She'd need to make a rope halter for Ghost and grab a tiki torch for light. Ghost would be back to his mom and she'd be back to the restaurant before anyone noticed she'd been gone.

A sudden wave of hunger made Hali double over in pain. Her muscles cramped and she pressed against her belly. An image of raw meat filled her mind.

"No, no, no." Hali straightened and glanced around. The sensation increased. Ghost was awake and looking for her.

She sprinted for Roni. The older girl caressed a tourist's arm, staring up at his face. He stared back, besotted, oblivious to the small bottle she poured into his drink with her other hand.

Hali pressed her lips together, recognizing the medicine to help people sleep.

Sliding between the tourist and Roni, Hali pulled on Roni's sleeve. "I need to talk to you. It's urgent."

Roni narrowed her eyes in anger, but she laughed towards the tourist as she twisted away with Hali.

"This had better be good." Roni pinched Hali's arm.

"It is. This guy over there," Hali waved her hand toward the perimeter, "says he can help me get the drone. He'll pay to rent a kayak and I'll take him out. If anything bad happens then you won't be affected, but if it works then I'll give you half. I just need the keys to the kayak."

Hunger pangs gnawed at Hali. "And freezer."

"Sounds like you need me more than half because I have the keys and you don't. Seventy-five percent." Roni's mouth twitched. "Why are you holding your stomach like that?"

"Agreed, but I need dinner first." Hali held out her hand. "Then I'll go."

"You're so weird." Roni shrugged. "Whatever. Both keys are on the set."

Hali, keys secured, veered toward the tourist who was watching Roni with a worried expression. Roni stared into the distance, apparently dreaming of what she'd do with the money.

"She'll be right back," Hali said. The tourist didn't look away from Roni as Hali switched their drinks and continued inside past the kitchen to the freezers.

"Hey!" One of the cooks yelled at her.

"It's for Roni," Hali called, waving the keys.

Scared that Ghost would appear any moment, Hali shoved raw meat into a bag and then dashed out the back door towards the kayaks stacked on the beach. Her hands shook as she twisted the key and the lock dropped to the sand.

Hali felt more than saw the pale colt hovering outside the tiki lamps.

"Come on, Lady Moon, I need a little help," Hali prayed as she loped around the perimeter to meet the colt. Seeing her, Ghost lifted his muzzle as if to nicker a greeting, but Hali tossed a hunk of raw meat toward the kelpie. His teeth glinted in the moonlight a moment before his mouth snapped closed. A gulp and the meat disappeared. Red dotted his muzzle.

Happiness surged through her. Hali smiled, bemused, and glanced inside the lit area. Dearie was still drinking with the tourists and Roni was halfway through the drink she'd medicated for her tourist. Ghost took a step toward her—or toward the sack of meat.

The net lights glowed red.

"Guess that's your answer, Lady Moon?" Hali's breath came fast; she had to keep control. There wasn't going to be a better time but she wasn't ready.

Holding the sack of meat, Hali sprinted toward the kayaks, trusting that Ghost would follow.

She tossed the sack into the bottom kayak and unthreaded the rope. Digging her heels into the loose sand she pushed the kayak off the rack towards shore. Damn, it was heavy and the rope stung her hands. Ghost wasn't helping. He was snuffling at the kayak and trying to get the meat. He thought this was a game.

"Stop it," she whispered. "Bad kelpie."

If anyone in the restaurant saw then the tourists would keep Ghost from his mother. Maybe they would put him on display and sell tickets to watch him eat. Maybe the Johnnies would declare war on the mainland. Maybe they wouldn't keep the sea eels away anymore.

Fear galvanized her. She shoved the kayak across the sand toward the water. It moved, inch by inch. Suddenly the weight lightened and Hali pitched forward onto her knees. Ghost had the rope in his mouth and backed up, pulling the kayak into the water. He didn't understand this game, but he wanted to help.

You're the smartest kelpie ever, she thought to Ghost.

Hali wiped her stinging hands on her shirt and jumped inside.

"Yummy dinner." She grabbed a hunk of meat and shook it. Sticky. Very sticky. "You know I'm a vegetarian, right?"

Ghost's hunger flared. He lifted his snout and snapped his teeth. She should be terrified of those teeth, but she was more scared of someone taking him away.

When Ghost was in the surf, Hali used the paddle to push off. Dip one side, then the other. She was going backwards into the waves in order to watch the kelpie colt swimming behind. There'd been no time to make a halter. And their guide through the water would have to be the island's righthand mast pole for the net, which hopefully still glowed red.

Ghost swam after her. *Thank you, Lady Moon, that no one at the restaurant noticed.* Two more strokes and the kayak came to an abrupt stop. The sandbar. Halfway to the main island. Hali used the stop to shift position in the kayak. Now she could see the net's light ahead, but Ghost would be behind her.

"Let's go find your mommy," she said, glancing over her shoulder.

The paddle slid through nerveless fingers and only the flipper's width prevented her from losing it in the water.

Torches lit up the beach. Figures poured from Dearie's restaurant with more torches. Feedback screamed as music was replaced by Dearie's voice: "The girl is in a kayak. Find her, but be careful with the drone. There's a reward if you bring them both to me."

Hali blinked as the figures on the beach pushed kayaks and boats that she'd left unlocked into the water. Roni must have told Dearie about the made-up plan—maybe when she realized the drugged drinks had been switched or maybe immediately? Regardless, she and Ghost were now being chased by drunk tourists.

Impatient for more meat, Ghost nosed at her hand.

Stomach churning from anxiety, Hali nodded her head, though it was too dark for the kelpie to see. "It's okay." It was not okay, but she had to get Ghost home.

Hali focused on the Johnnie's light and paddled toward it. So she saw immediately when it flickered green and then went back to red. What did that mean? A bitter laugh escaped. What else could go wrong?

Her comm sent a shock up her arm. Dearie was trying to pinpoint her location. If Dearie hadn't been so drunk, she would have thought of it sooner. Panicked, Hali held the side buttons down. That turned off her comm, but Dearie would be able to override it as soon as she got into the office. What would this do to her contract? Hali wiped her left arm across her eyes. She couldn't go back to Dearie's, not after tonight. Hali's breath hitched. Any minute Dearie was going to figure out exactly where she was. There was no way to keep a secret when you had a comm. She stared at the technology, familiar to her as any part of her own body. HER ENTIRE LIFE WAS ON THE COMM. And she would give it up to protect Ghost.

She bit the side strap. Her teeth worried at the material, but made no impact. Then Ghost was there, standing on the sandbar, summoned by her fear. His head butted at her and his little hoofs clunked against the kayak as he tried to get close enough. Trusting, Hali held out her wrist to a creature bred to kill unseels. His baby teeth sliced through the strap.

Scared, Hali stared as the moonlight reflected off the broken strap. She could go back and get it repaired. Nothing here that couldn't be undone with another decade of service to some new contractor. Ghost dipped his head, trusting her to make the right decision. No other being—human or otherwise—had ever done that. Hali worked her fingers underneath the comm, closed her eyes, and pulled. The tines slid out in unhurried ease. Random electric shocks ran up her arm and made her teeth vibrate. Then, with a sucking sound, it was out. Only the tail left to go.

Hali shuddered against Ghost. He held steady, letting her lean. Her fingers couldn't gain purchase so she used her teeth to fasten on the strap still connected to the tail. Blinded by tears, Hali gave into little moans of pain. Love and pride competed inside her—a message from Ghost. Hali wiped her nose against Ghost's mane and then bit the strap again as she pulled her arm towards her ribcage. The tail was harder than the tines, the scar tissue unwilling to yield. Hali screamed around the bit in her mouth—the strap of the comm—but didn't stop pulling. And when it finally yanked free, crimson flowed down her arm and she sagged against Ghost.

Ghost took the comm and bit it, letting the pieces fall into the water.

Then an image of meat popped into her mind. Hali laughed as she wiped her tears.

"Why, yes. You do get a treat for that." Good thing she'd grabbed so much meat. At least that was going right. Hali balanced the paddle on her knees while she pulled a section apart. The paddle slipped as the kayak rocked. Were those ripples from the kayaks near shore?

"Ghost!"

She shook the meat, but the kelpie had swum away from the sandbar to face Nursery Island.

"Wrong island, buddy. We've gotta meet your mom and we need to hurry."

Suddenly, an alarm split the air, shrieking across the water from the main island. The net lights blinked red, off and on. The net had been breached.

A sea monster was in the bay.

Adrenaline pumping, Hali thrust her paddle into the water but a huge wave hit from the side. Seawater soaked her clothes, drenching her hair and burning her eyes. The kayak tipped. Hali rose to her knees and grabbed onto the side, clawing for a handhold so she wouldn't be dumped into the freezing water. The sack of meat slid down. She let go with one hand and stretched, reaching for the bag. Her fingers touched just as another wave knocked into the kayak and spun it around.

Got it! Her fingers clutched the sack.

The kayak righted and Hali held the bottom of the empty sack. She could only watch as chunks of meat descended into the water, imagine the smell diffusing and summoning.

Holy Lady Moon, what have I done?

The kayak kept rocking.

I've lured an unseel straight toward us.

Hali thrust her paddle into the water and shot forward toward the main island. Maybe they could make it. "Come on, Ghost!"

He continued facing away from her.

Resolution with a hint of fierce joy. A burst of love.

Hali's chest constricted. Ghost wanted to defend her. He wasn't going to run because he wanted to fight the unseel. That's what he'd been bred to do, but he didn't realize he was only a baby.

Ghost's little white head bobbed in the moonlight, his sharp baby teeth exposed as if that would scare away the monster. Splashing in the distance as the stupid tourists reacted to the alarm.

No more good plans existed. Only one truth: she wasn't leaving Ghost.

He lifted his muzzle and let out a coltish imitation of the black stallion's whinny from earlier.

Hali stroked toward Ghost through the choppy water.

"I'm coming, Ghost." She reached for his tufts of mane and patted the kayak. "Get in." His weight would probably sink them both, but she wasn't going to let him be attacked from below.

He tried, kicking the kayak with a hoof, but it wasn't going to work and she wasn't going to save him.

"I love you," she said. One day with Ghost had been worth more than anything else in her life.

Ripples from the unseel zigzagged toward the kayak, highlighted by the moonlight.

Ghost lifted his muzzle to scream again, but it wasn't his voice that rang out. It was a mother kelpie's voice that shattered the moonlight as she splashed into the water from the main island.

Hali gaped as Johnnies, mounted on kelpies, charged from the island. Torches flickered into light, revealing kelpies swimming through the cold dark water in ordered ranks, splitting around her and Ghost, the charge led by Ghost's mother.

"Get out of the way," a Johnnie yelled as she rode past.

"Ghost! You have to get my colt."

A different rider swam past her toward the island, the white colt across the kelpie's haunches.

Hali followed. When the kayak hit sand, Hali stumbled out and ran to the rider, helping Ghost slide to the beach.

The alarm continued to blare, and Hali wanted to cover her ears, but instead she wrapped her arms around Ghost's neck. A mountain of water poured down in buckets as a smooth body reared up from the water, no eyes, but a mouth opening to reveal circular rows of teeth. Kelpies spread into a defensive line while their Johnnies wielded long spears.

The unseel, spears hanging out of its body, ignored the soldiers.

"Grab the harpoon," the rider beside Hali yelled. "The unseel has tasted blood and won't turn." Another Johnnie ran inland.

With a giant splash, the unseel bellyflopped into the water, its back fin headed straight toward the island. Its long, streamlined body outpaced the chasing kelpies.

The rider grabbed Hali's arm and pulled her, holding onto Ghost, up the beach until their backs were against the rocky wall of the canyon.

The unseel rose straight up from the water, weaving back and forth like a snake, and then flung its body into the sand, mouth gaping open only a few feet from the rider, Hali, and Ghost. Hot, fetid breath covered them. They were trapped. Each tooth was as long as Hali's forearm; they shined like daggers in the mix of moonlight and torches.

Rocks cut Hali's back as she pressed back and her hands dug into Ghost's mane. The Johnnie pulled out a saber, but the blade was the same length as the unseel's tooth.

Ghost screamed a challenge again.

A metallic clanging from the side suggested the harpoon was being adjusted, but it would be too late to keep the unseel away from Ghost. They needed more time.

The unseel surged forward, but Hali pushed herself away from the wall, arms outstretched. "Hey, Moonface!"

Teeth ripped into her right arm. The bone snapped. Hali was lifted off her feet, body hanging from the unseel until it shook its head. Hali's flesh ripped and she fell to the sand, hard.

Pain exploded. Hali screamed, grabbing her mutilated arm with her left hand and writhing in the sand. Fire spread from her ruined arm to her chest, to her stomach. Panic. She couldn't see, couldn't stop shaking, couldn't breathe from the impact.

And then a different warmth was there. Ghost. Pain still burned, panic still lodged in her throat; but, somehow, he filtered them.

The eel reared to the side, shaking back and forth.

There was a break in the canyon wall—entrance to the Johnnie's stronghold. She had to crawl there.

With a whoosh, the harpoon launched.

The unseel shook itself again and then curved around to bite at its own body.

The distraction gave enough time for the herd of kelpies to surge from the sea, the water horses biting at the eel, tearing away flesh with their own predator's teeth, and finishing the kill. Slowly, too slowly, the unseel uncurved and its mouth hit the sand, jaw opening on impact to release the body of a grey mare with white spots and a dark mane and tail. Her teeth were flecked with blood and flesh, clenched around the dorsal fin like an enemy's banner.

She'd attacked from behind. That's why the eel had curved away. That's why Hali had been dropped. The mare's attack had saved their group.

The Johnnie thrust her saber into the scabbard. "Close the nets," she yelled. Then she pivoted to stare down at Hali. "You. Start explaining." It was the rear rider—the one who been so disdainful toward Mainlanders.

"Ghost got left behind," Hali said, as cold spread through her body. The sand had turned into a pillow and she was melting into it. Was this shock? Ghost nosed her side in concern. "I tried to bring him back. Everything is my fault."

Riders moved along the beach pulling spears from the eel while the kelpies formed a circle around the dead mare. Ghost's mother.

"This young woman, Cavalier Felis, saved one of our colts." New torchlight revealed an older man approaching. Overgrown eyebrows shadowed kind eyes. "And, unless I'm wrong, she imprinted with him."

"No," Felis said, folding her arms. "Mainlanders can't imprint." She added, "Doctor Dramock."

"Perhaps we should ask—did you say 'Ghost'—what he thinks." Dramock rubbed Ghost's neck in a complicated pattern.

Runes glowed in blue swirls. Emotions pulsed through Hali: acceptance, trust, and love.

"Impossible." Felis sputtered in outrage. "That would change everything."

"Perhaps it's time." Dramock knelt beside Hali and pushed something against her neck. Sensation and then relief. "This will help, but you need surgery."

Hali's teeth chattered, but she managed: "Ghost's mother died because of me."

"Ghost's mother died because she is a soldier and a sea monster attacked. She protected her colt and the humans around him. We will accord her the highest honor at a bonfire at the next full moon." He glanced up. "Indeed, the ripples of tonight will have many effects."

As Dramock readied the stretcher, Felis stalked into the darkness. Other riders walked past into the canyon, but the kelpies crooned over their lost comrade, sad, shifting tones that plucked Hali's heart. Ghost pushed forward into the herd; the kelpies greeted him with their noses. Hali closed her eyes as the song from the water horses rose to the moon in tribute and memorial.

Publication History

"Bake Me a Cake" new for this collection

"Child of Moon and Sea", *Abyss & Apex Magazine*, 2014

"Breakage", *Abyss & Apex Magazine*, 2018

"My Own Skin", *Once Upon a Dystopia: An Anthology of Twisted Fairy Tales and Fractured*

Folklore, 2021

"A Quick Getaway", *Pantheon Magazine*, 2018

"At the Night Bazaar", *Black-Eyed Peas on New Year's Day: An Anthology of Hope*, 2021

"Saving Money", *Flash Fiction Magazine*, 2015

"1416 DeForested Lane", *Pantheon Magazine*, 2016

"The Great Blockage" new for this collection

"Monsters Beautiful and Bright", *DreamForge Magazine*, 2020

"Boy from Omran", *Pantheon Magazine*, 2018

"Mama Salamander", *Spaceports & Spidersilk*, 2015

"Finders Keepers", *Love and Other Dangers*, 2023

"An Excuse, An Invitation Even", *Orpheus + Eurydice Unbound*, 2022

"Swan Dive", *Musings of the Muses*, 2022

"Where the Kelpies Swim", *Abyss & Apex Magazine*, 2025

Story Notes

"**Bake Me a Cake**" is a mixture (excuse the pun) of watching *The Great British Baking Show* with my family during Covid lockdown and writing a submission for a Tanith Lee tribute anthology that draws on the idea of Christina Rossetti's poem "Goblin Market" (1862).

"**Child of Moon and Sea**" is my first semi-pro sale and it started a wonderful relationship with *Abyss & Apex Magazine*.

"**Breakage**" is an exploration of being both empathetic and society teaching us to hide our pain.

"**My Own Skin**" is a science fiction version of the selkie myth in which a seal-woman is robbed of her pelt.

"**A Quick Getaway.**" Doesn't everyone think of state fairs and funnel cakes and wasp queens when they imagine summer?

"**At the Night Bazaar**" is a fan favorite and the response really encouraged me. As usual, the whimsical elements make some people ask if this is a children's story. This makes me think of how fairy tales are so often thought of in the same way—children's stories—when the original versions are dark, sexual, and violent.

"**Saving Money**" and "**1416 DeForested Lane**" both came out of a time period when we were looking for a new house. My older daughter loved the props—the glass of plastic wine, the bow across the toilet so it wouldn't be used, the board games set up as if someone had just walked away. I was disturbed by the beautiful trees being cut down for "progress" and wondered about the supernatural creatures who might object to their habitat being destroyed.

"The Great Blockage" is another attempt to wrestle with how recycling is too often a glib solution when, in fact, several factors keep it from being effective in its current form.

"Monsters Beautiful and Bright" is a play on the story of Hansel and Gretel.

"Boy from Omran" is a tribute to the courage it takes to leave a place when it becomes unsafe, trusting that you will find something better. It started from the spark of LeGuin's "The Ones Who Walk Away from Omelos" but morphed into its own iteration.

"Mama Salamander." One of my children had a rough day at school. This story was the result.

"Finders Keepers" features characters from The Misbegotten series (published under the pseudonym Searby Gray) after the events of the novel.

"An Excuse, An Invitation Even" is a retelling of the Orpheus and Eurydice myth, but only the beginning and set in the American West in the 1850's. The complete book from Air and Nothingness Press, *O + E Unbound*, pieces together stories from different authors to tell the entire tale, switching genres and time periods with each story.

"Swan Dive" is another Greek myth (Leda and the swan) retelling and introduces a character who plays a role in my current novel-in-progress about the Greek gods. The twist is that this story is told from Leda's point of view rather than Zeus's.

"Where the Kelpies Swim" is the latest story that I've placed with *Abyss & Apex Magazine*. I love the way this market allows a mix of fantasy and sci-fi, as long as it suits the story.

About the Author

Sherri Cook Woosley holds a master's degree in English Literature with a focus on comparative mythology from the University of Maryland. She's a SFWA member, and her short fiction has been published in *O+E Unbound, Abyss & Apex Magazine,* and *Dreamforge Magazine.* Her debut novel, WALKING THROUGH FIRE (Talos Press, 2018), was long-listed for both the Booknest Debut Novel award and nominated for Baltimore's Best 2019 and 2020 in the novel category. Her speculative mystery novelette *Mother's Instinct* was released by eSpec Books in fall 2024.

Her first children's book, *Postcards from a City of Monsters,* is based on her Pushcart-nominated short story "Gargoyles in Prague." The children's book was published by Improbable Press in August 2024 and won a Mom's Choice Gold Award in 2025.

About the Illustrator

This book is Joshua Ormido's debut as an illustrator. He honed his skills in advanced art classes and is currently studying at University of Maryland. In his free time, Joshua has competed, and won awards, for identifying trees and flowers. He invites anyone to challenge him to an arboreal genus and species quiz.